HEAVEN'S GENERATION

LAURENT GAIDEN

authorHOUSE®

AuthorHouse™
1663 Liberty Drive, Suite 200
Bloomington, IN 47403
www.authorhouse.com
Phone: 1-800-839-8640

First published by AuthorHouse 8/25/2009

ISBN: 978-1-4389-7229-9 (sc)

Printed in the United States of America
Bloomington, Indiana

This book is printed on acid-free paper.

This is a writing exercise.
I hope I get some comments on it. Let me know what you think.

Enjoy!

Behold, you give me a devil of creation and I shall give you an angel of destruction.

-*Anonymous*

A NIGHT IN PARADISE

A PRIEST CAME TO THE MIDDLE OF THE WALKWAY, KNELT down on one knee, and put his hands together. Thunder was roaring, but he ignored it. The man was Peter Adams, a respected man of his community, a part of Greenwood's Paradise.

On this night, he was alone. He liked to be alone at times. It was a way to communicate better with his Lord. His mind would be reconditioned whenever he was alone and those were his brightest moments.

This was an unusual night, however. Things were lurking in the night and dangerous forces were prowling. He was uneasy as he was thinking.

"Dear Lord," Peter said to himself, "Sometimes I feel that I will do a special service for you. I would like you to know that if this is the destiny I must go, then guide me, Lord, and I will happily sacrifice myself to show my allegiance."

Footsteps were heard. The priest got up from the floor quickly and looked around.

"Who's there? Show yourself!"

A hooded, shadowy person came out from the seats and walked up the middle to him. He started clapping slowly. Unknown to Peter, a second hooded person was on top of a cross hanging above him.

"Nice prayer, Priest," the first hood said. "Too bad it will be your last."

"What do you want?"

"Your head," the second hood said from above. "What else?"

The first hood was now a few feet close to him. "The woman? Where is she? If you tell us, maybe we'll let you live."

Priest stood confident. "Then you might as well take my life, you devils. I'll protect them with my life."

"Wrong answer!"

The second hood jumped down and attacked Peter. Peter defended himself against his first attacker, but then, the other hood dropped down and stabbed Peter with his rapier. Peter fell to the ground dead and the second hood stabbed him with their knife a few more times before disappearing into the air.

* * *

Gladiator brawls were the sport of champions for Greenwood. It symbolized power and grace. Fans were cheering for the respected teams and cheerleaders were cheering for the stimulation of life.

None had greater champions that the college towns Sodom and Gomorrah, located near the downtown area of the Tri-Cities.

Other towns, large and small, were forming, but some remain the same for the sake of remembering the past, a time where the world was in trouble and it was fixed in a blaze of fire. As for the students of the respected colleges, few passed and moved up to become priests, philosophers, or prophets while others become soldiers, generals, or celebrities.

Sodom College's champion, Thorn Hawkins, came into the ring with lethal intentions. He was in for the fight of his life. It was for the Collegiate Championship and his opponent, Roberto Ruiz, had twenty straight defenses. No one was able to take him down. Thorn had trained hard just for this chance and he was going to get it.

As soon as the bell rang, he came out swinging and Roberto was there to counterattack. In the first round of thirteen, Thorn knocked him out. It was a slight sting, but it was when Roberto got up that Thorn smelled blood and was trying to end the fight quickly with a knockout.

The next four rounds were just like this. Thorn's intensity could be felt among the stands of Sodom Stadium. Thorn was an underdog going into the fight, but the fans of Sodom had complete faith in their champion.

However, in the sixth round, Roberto found an opening and exploited it. He got Thorn cleaned in the head and Thorn was on the defensive. Seeing that he was about to win, he went in for the kill. The bell saved Thorn from getting massacred. In the next three rounds, Roberto was in control. Thorn knew that he had to muster everything he had to win this fight. Sodom fans gave him the energy he needed and without warning, Thorn found an opening in the body and attacked it. Then, like a wild beast, he ferociously attacked Roberto, getting another knockout. As soon as Roberto got up, Thorn knew that he had the fight and went in to finish it. The referee held on to Thorn before he killed Roberto.

His fans started cheering their loudest. He waved his fist in the air in triumph, waving to the people who were proud of him. And they were proud of this young man. This young man had a bright future ahead of him, no matter what he did, others were thinking. Especially one of the cheerleaders, Cecilia Broughton, who came into the ring and kissed her passionately.

Thorn and Cecilia was the perfect couple of Sodom College, the football player who loved to play because of the challenge and the cheerleader who liked nothing better than to boast about how brave her boyfriend was. They were complete opposites of each other, but it only enhanced the relationship. Other Sodom students made great, romantic stories about them, seeing them as star-crossed.

Both were young, with Thorn being slightly older than Cecilia. Both were opposites. Both were so much in love.

Thorn Hawkins was the perfect example of what, in most priests' eyes, what Jehovah wanted and needed from his fellow children. But Thorn tried his best not to associate himself with those rumors or rumors of any kind, unlike Cecilia, a mysterious girl with many secrets that she was not proud of having and was willing to follow Thorn's God to escape them. She was under the scrutiny of rumors every day. Thorn tried his best to stay away from the mystery of her past, but sometimes, it was hard to hide because they were always coming at him from all directions.

To Cecilia, Thorn was the only person in the world who would give her a chance, and she tried her best to be the dutiful woman, almost becoming completely subservient to him. It had gotten as far as total submission. Cecilia wanted to please him, so she could please herself. One disadvantage that stuck with her was her towering sex drive that arose whenever she was around him. Ever since she was little she had been a victim of it until she became the slave to seduction. She was hoping that not only Thorn could be the benevolent man she loved, but be the sexual creature that would stop the friction of her hormones.

Thorn Hawkins never wanted to be the popular or the strong-armored type. Growing up with priests, he was once a quiet boy. Sensing how the priests did their work, studying the Word of the Lord as well as the ways of the Old World and the mistakes that had been made, he desired to become one of them. He wanted to learn the world of learning about the mistake of the past.

But a build up of muscle and a close encounter with death changed all of it.

One day, when Thorn was reaching his pre-teens, a small-time hood, probably was a devil apprentice, was kicking a fellow boy no older than he was. The reason was unknown to him, as was the identity of the hood, but Thorn saved the child's life, knowing by that moment, his life was at risk. He made sure that no child would ever be hurt again. With this came the workouts, the participation in sports, and a build up of confidence that made him leave the world of the priests forever and enter the realm of the soldiers. Thorn knew he had the mental ability to survive, but he wanted to move more with his body, and in the realm of the soldiers, he knew that he could master his strength as well as his mental capacity. He loved the power the soldiers carry. In becoming a soldier came battle, and with his muscles building up, Thorn wanted battles. He wanted nothing more than to prove himself, which was a reason he became a gladiator fighter.

Thorn walked to the car as he told his friends goodbye, wearing his trademark jacket with insignia of angel wings on it. Cecilia went to him, gave him a kiss and got in on the passenger side. They drove off to the street. They got further away from the school and into the shadows of night. Thorn was concentrating on the road while Cecilia was concentrating on her boyfriend, who was looking delectable to her.

"Are you sure you're okay?" Cecilia asked, still wandering about the impact from the blows given in the ring.

"Why are you still asking me that?" Thorn asked. "I told you I'm fine."

Thorn was still feeling the effect, but he knew how to hide it. It started from his back and managed to reach his shoulder blades.

"I mean you took a good hit trying to make that touchdown," Cecilia said. "I don't see why you take risks like that."

"Comes with the territory," Thorn said.

"Well, I get scared sometimes when you take those hits. But you know, those hits you take… kind of… well…"

Cecilia took Thorn's hand and put it on her chest. She moved Thorn's hand around her breasts, making his hand squeeze them a little. Cecilia loved to be frisky to Thorn. He was a handsome man with a sex appeal most women, good or evil, adored.

"What are you doing?" Thorn asked irritated.

"What you think?" Cecilia asked sensually.

Cecilia went down to his waist and started unzipping his pants. She could tell upon touching him that he was throbbing. He was feeling it as well. Suddenly, Thorn stopped the car abruptly to a corner. He gently pushed Cecilia off of him.

"What's wrong?" Cecilia said angrily to Thorn and gave him a shove for ruining another good mood.

"It's not right," Thorn said. "I don't want you to do that."

"Oh, great, don't tell you going to get modest again."

"I told you about that. I respect you very well, Cecilia, and I want this to be good."

"And… me wanting to make love to my man is a problem?"

"You're better than that."

Cecilia did not like when Thorn started acting benevolent and caring.

"That's a first," she said.

"I love you," Thorn said. "I want you to be who you are. You don't have to please me. I'm already pleased. And the Lord is pleased as well."

"You're bringing God into this?"

"Look, I'll just take you home and we'll talk about this later."

"Fine. Whatever you want?"

Cecilia crossed her arms in disappointment. Thorn started the car and drove off. Another night of romance ruined by sacred duty.

* * *

A figure stood with a cloak on and a hood over his head, looking out into the night. He looked up and saw the stars. His cloak, mixed with the black and blue of the night, made him looked majestic. This was a usual hobby. Sometimes the person would look up at the sky and images would fly around in their head.

At other times, there was nothing. Nothing but the night and the stars.

Jumping from one roof to another before finally reaching the roof where the cloaked person was, the two hooded persons from the church walked to him. Without even looking at them, he could tell that they had a wonderful time.

"It's done," the first hooded person said. "We found the priest. He didn't know where the woman was."

"However," the second cut in, "we had a problem. He put up a fight and we… killed him."

"So where do we go from here?"

The figure turned and looked at his comrades in the corner of his eye. The two hooded persons saw the bone and skull. The hooded persons stared scarily at him and started to back away. They knew that this was not a good time. Perhaps, he already knew what went on and didn't care.

Perhaps!

* * *

The liveliest club around the Tri-Cities was Club Lucifer, where sin was active and everyone had a taste. A party was going on at the club with crazy, seductive dancing and heavy drinking from the dance floor and topside, even among the large stairs they have. In cages, they were strippers and exhibitionists doing their duties to excite, all taking pride in their performances. Unfortunately, despite it being the Tri-Cities, there were still some renegade devils and lost souls around that wanted nothing better than to create or seek sin.

Watching from a window of a room was the owner, Dmitri Sheppard. Dmitri was known for the dark arts, could master and decipher moves anyone threw his direction. No one messed with Dmitri and his Underground Devils, soldiers fighting for what others thought of as a lost cause. Dmitri was known as the true Prince of Devils. One thing that differed between the two was the viciousness without thinking in Dmitri.

Dmitri has always lived life rough, never anticipating the moments in which he had the chance to show what he did. He grew up with street rats. No parents, siblings, and no shoulder to cry on but each other's. He knew of the stories of the ongoing battle between angels and devils. Priests and preachers who either knew better or wanted a profit had told it to him in different forms. His belief in the Prince of Devils, although unhealthy, had got him through the treacherous times. With these old friends, he started the Underground Devils, whose main mission was to embrace the word of the "wicked one." If they were ever on trial, they defended their word by telling others that the Wicked One was robbed of his right for being wrongly accused.

Dmitri lived the life of the scavenger. He loved being compared to a rat, his symbol. The rat was a scavenger of the land, who never regretted his nature of being a thief, especially taking things no one care about. Plus, the rat was so small he could go through anything to escape danger, in which Dmitri also could do. Nothing or no one could touch him.

Suddenly, someone came into the club, wearing a stylish white suit, and lots of jewelry, showboating with the best of them. It irritated Dmitri a little, but because that was the way he was, plus he was a regular at Club Lucifer, Dmitri dealt with it. Not only was he a regular, he was the main star. As he paraded around the club, all handed out their hands as if looking for handouts. He even went to the strippers and dancers inside the cage. No one, including Dmitri, didn't expect anything else from the likes of Vegas Armano.

Vegas Armano was known for his internal rebellious nature. No one knew why Vegas was rebellious or what constitute to his behavior, but they dealt with it. Vegas was always about making his own moves, not listening to authority, which complicated things for teachers of the faith.

Vegas saw Dmitri and shrugged. He showed the suitcase he was carrying. He walked forward, moving people smoothly out of his way.

Vegas was invited to V.I.P by a guard. Dmitri came in and the two shook hands. He saw Dmitri's friends, having a good time, with the exception of one. He sat still, in a thinking position, not caring about the excitement, as if he wanted to go someplace else, but afraid to go. He was Giorgio Martel, a young devil amateur working for Dmitri. Another character was looking at Giorgio. He was another devil amateur named Cosine Secant. Vegas stared at Cosine.

"Vegas, I was waiting all night for you," Dmitri said.

"It'll be worth the wait," Vegas said. "Trust me."

"So show me."

Vegas opened the suitcase and took it out. It was a package of a drug with the code name *manna*, which was a drug craze to the teenagers of the Tri-Cities. It was said to enhance the sin of humans ten times it was worth. Vegas stared at the insignia of an imitation devil on the package, the color red, horns, and a gruesome face. Vegas thought it was best to decorate the bag for him to ensure him of his good graces, even though he knew better. He knew that devils were the most seductive creatures around because they played on intellect, or lack thereof.

Vegas gestured with his hands. "The greatest *manna* in the world. Better than any brand."

Dmitri knew of Vegas' cockiness. "Of course you have the best. I'm just surprised your boss doesn't have something to say about it."

"Let's just say that my boss and I aren't on speaking terms," Vegas said. "And as far as I'm concerned, I'm not into patience."

"Well, you can always come to the winning side. Let's face it, you wouldn't be in the business if it wasn't for me."

"I'm okay by myself."

"Fine with me. And as a present for coming through…"

Dmitri snapped his fingers. "Hope you like it."

Vegas looked at two women coming to him. They started caressing him. Dmitri knew how to impress.

"There's a room to the left for privacy," Dmitri said and pointed to the door to the room.

Vegas went with the women to the room.

Suddenly, gunshots were heard. Dmitri went to see what was going on. The Angel Guards were in the building. They took people out the club. One of them stared at Dmitri looking out the window and started to run.

Dmitri and his gang took out their things and started running out to their secret exit. One of the guards came in with his gun and saw an empty room. The cop was Shadow Fears. He looked around and heard sounds of laughter. He went slowly to where the noise was as it got higher and higher. He found the door and broke it open. He pointed the gun at a naked Vegas and the two girls. The girls ran off and Shadow put his gun in his back pocket.

"Vegas Armano," Shadow said. "What the hell are you doing at a place like this?"

Vegas gave a smirk. "Having fun. What you think?"

"Hanging among devils now? You really reach a low."

"And who the hell are you? Oh, I forgot, a spy."

"I'm not spying on you. I was here for your friends, but apparently they split before I could reach them."

Vegas smiled. "Like you was going to catch Dmitri anyway. He's too slick for you. They all are."

Shadow was aggravated. "Get out of here."

Vegas got his clothes and strolled off naked. Shadow looked at the two near-intersecting lines on Vegas's back where his angel wings were. *How in the world did God accept him,* Shadow thought.

A fellow agent went to Shadow. "Shadow! We got a call. Turns out Priest Adams was murdered."

Shadow was shocked. He knew of the benevolence of Priest Adams and anyone would have killed for that was on his hit list.

"When was this?" Shadow asked.

"They say it's been a while. They got agents there now at the church."

"We didn't get Dmitri and now this. Let's go."

* * *

Agents surrounded the dead body of Peter Adams. Shadow came in with other agents. He went on his knees to get a closer look.

"Any evidence?" Shadow asked.

The first agent came to him. "None so far. We think that it could have been a robbery attempt."

"Check around to see if anything's missing."

Shadow looked around.

A second agent came to Shadow. "What you think?"

Shadow looked up at the cross. He pointed to it.

"The cross up there," Shadow said as he pointed, making a trace of the cross. "It looks a little edgy, which means the killer was on top of it. Which also means that the killer was not that heavy. Jumps down and attacks Priest from this spot."

Shadow pointed at the spot. The agents stared at it, then at every move Shadow made. Whenever Shadow explained things like this, other agents followed it like a play.

"But there was a struggle," Shadow said. "He fought back. However, turn him over."

An agent turned Priest's body over, in which there were stab wounds on his back.

Shadow continued. "Stab wounds on the back, which could mean that there were two killers. The first one attacks him on the back, Priest falls, the second finishes the job, and they fly away. Very good! Get him out of here. We have to figure out how we're going to tell the public."

Shadow watched as Priest's body was taken away. Shadow looked around again and something caught his eye. It was a small silver skull. He looked at it carefully.

It can't be who I think it is.

* * *

A car rode down the street as fast as it could.

Dmitri and his friends drove as far away from the club as possible. This was not typical for Dmitri. Usually, he dealt with the harassment from the agents trying to take down his businesses and his gang. He respected the agents for their duties, but his gang did not.

The car stopped at a sign that showed the direction to the Tri-Cities, one leading to Sodom and the other heading to Jerusalem. One of the devils opened the car door to let Giorgio out.

"Look," Dmitri said to Giorgio, "if those agents come see you to ask you where I am…"

Giorgio stopped him. "Don't worry. I don't know you."

"You did well, kid."

They drove off with the same speed and Giorgio started running.

Giorgio managed to sneak into a room of a house from the window quietly. He closed the window. He stared at a woman sleeping: his lover Robin Jenkins. He went to her and kissed her on the cheek. Robin felt it, but did not open her eyes. He went to the bed and lay near her. She turned to caress him.

"Where were you?" Robin whispered. "I was worried."

Giorgio was insecure talking with Robin about his dealings with Dmitri. She was a delicate person that did not deserve to even look at someone like him.

"Had to take care of something," Giorgio said. "Make sure things are set."

"You don't have to be out there, you know," Robin said.

"Then, what else are we going to do? We have to make ends meet. I almost got caught."

"Not those men with the—"

"Not them. Although I'm sure they out there trying to find us."

"We can't continue to hide from them, whatever is after us."

"This is only temporary until something better comes up. This will be behind us. No one is going to harm us. I'll make sure of that."

Giorgio went and kissed Robin on the forehead. "I love you."

"I love you, too."

THE TRI-CITIES

SODOM COLLEGE WAS THE MOST LUXURIOUS OF THE SCHOOLS IN Greenwood. The architects and designers put their heads together and told themselves that they would make this school just as majestic as Greenwood's other college temples. However, the plans went further and the one temple became a college town.

In their golden halls, which mirrored the great view of the blue sky showing the bright day in its texture, Vegas Armano and Thorn Hawkins walked together and conversed, while acknowledging fellow students. Despite their differences in views and beliefs, Vegas and Thorn respected one another. It was that respect that became the basis of their strong friendship.

"How was it with Cecilia?" Vegas said, joking around.

"She wanted to have sex with me," Thorn said.

Vegas looked strangely at Thorn. He knew of Cecilia with her good looks and wild sexual appetite. He was surprised that she went for a focused student like Thorn. Cecilia was not that type, Vegas was thinking. She was a freak, like he was.

"Damn," Vegas remarked. "She wanted to have sex with you? And what did you do?"

"I said no," Thorn said calmly.

"You said no?"

"Of course I said no. Don't get me wrong. I love Cecilia, but I just didn't want to do that with her."

Vegas knew there was an angle. "I tell you one thing, if she was my girlfriend and she wanted to make love, you think I'll say no?"

"I bet you won't."

Vegas stopped walking and touched Thorn's shoulder.

"You know what your problem is?" he asked. "You're too modest for this world. Like you fight in the ring, you need to be that for this life. You need to be cruel sometimes. That's the only way you're going to survive. I mean you think this new generation is any different than the old one."

"You mean you want me to be like you," Thorn said and gave a small laugh. "A criminal? I heard about you getting caught by the Guards at Club Lucifer. Working with Dmitri."

Thorn always had something against Vegas working with Dmitri or even making deals with him. Vegas only saw it as getting by. Thorn knew of Dmitri, but only through rumors and from those, he made up his mind that he didn't want to know about Dmitri. Vegas knew Dmitri, a lot more than imagined.

"And how do you know?" Vegas asked.

"People talk," Thorn said.

"Well, let them talk. I can give a care."

Thorn knew this. "What was you doing hanging with Dmitri anyway?"

A pause.

"Had to handle business for somebody," Vegas said.

"Who and what?" Thorn asked.

"Can't say. You'll know soon enough. By the way, guess who I also saw with Dmitri?"

"Who?"

"Cosine."

Cosine Secant. The mention of his brother from Vegas' mouth, Thorn knew something was up.

"You saw Cosine there?" Thorn asked. "What was he doing there?"

"Same thing I was doing. He and a bunch of other punks. What's this world coming to?"

Vegas looked over at another person, looking forward as other students were walking by, staring hard at him. Vegas stared at him as well. Vegas knew this student named Victor Marcus. Thorn looked at Vegas. The fun that was in his voice before suddenly turned cold at the glimpse of Victor.

"Vegas, what's wrong?" Thorn asked concerned.

Vegas took his time to answer. "Nothing… Just… wandering."

Thorn stared at Victor, as if he was hypnotized. "Who is that?"

Vegas was trying his best to take his eyes off of him, but he couldn't. It had a hypnotic tone on them. Finally, he said, "That's just Victor Marcus. Just some weirdo. Nobody important."

Thorn and Vegas walked on. Victor stared at Thorn and Vegas walking, step by step.

Walk on, you two, Victor thought. *Forget you know me. Soon enough, you're going to be helping me.*

* * *

Dmitri was with some of his crew at the club, which acted as hideout and praying center. Among some of the gang were Cosine Secant, Giorgio Martel, Essence Malone, one of the lethal females of the gang, and Larisa Rhodes, a young sultry beauty of the group.

Larisa shot herself with *manna* with a needle and with help from Essence. Most of the gang used it to enhance their adrenaline and sexual drive. Giorgio looked on, trying to fit in, but mostly, trying to hide. Dmitri did some tricks with his hand, a hobby he did often whenever he was thinking of schemes. He took some cards and made them disappear and reappear quickly or he would make the entire deck turned around him like the rotation of the Earth.

Cosine looked at him with admiration. "That's tight, Dmitri. When will I learn that?"

"You want to learn this?" Dmitri asked, amazed at his curiosity and enthusiasm. "You think you can handle it? You know what I think? I think it would kill you learning this."

Essence said, "Let him learn if he wants to. I think he can handle it."

"Of course you'll think so, would you? Well, I tell you what. We'll see if you got it, young one. We'll see if you and Giorgio have it. If you do, then we'll talk about those powers. If you want proof from me, I must have it in return. Giorgio knows, right?"

Giorgio got up after a few seconds pause. Larisa, who saw this, got up, thanks to a small push from Essence. Dmitri looked on as well.

Giorgio was on the phone with someone. Usually, he took time whenever the rest of the gang was busy to call Robin. Hearing her voice was the only thing that made him take whatever Dmitri dished out.

"Do not worry, darling," Giorgio whispered. "I'll take care of things. It's going a little slow, but for now we have to let it go slow. Besides, I don't want Dmitri or anyone else getting suspicious about our activities." He started hearing footsteps. "Someone's coming. I have to go. I love you."

Giorgio put up his phone. Larisa walked to him as Giorgio turned to her.

"What the hell was that all about in there?" Larisa asked.

Giorgio rubbed his head. "What are you talking about, Larisa?"

"Don't give me that bullshit! You know exactly what I'm talking about. Leaving out like that."

"Is it bad enough I can't think my thoughts among Dmitri and the rest of them, but now I have to hear about it from you?"

"Sorry! I didn't mean to be like that. I didn't think you would take it so hard. If it's any constellation, I never had any problem with you thinking."

Larisa's language turned sensual. "In fact, that's one of the main things I love about you,".

With Giorgio's back turn, Larisa put her arms around his waist. She caressed his chest. From this, she revealed the sacred mark on his chest, showing that he was an amateur devil. Giorgio walked away.

"I can't do this now," he said.

Larisa tried to stop him with her arm. "You never stop me before."

"Maybe that's my problem. I never tried to stop myself. But that's going to end. For now on, I'll have better control over myself."

Giorgio walked away. In his mind, he was thinking why he was cursed with the blessed attractiveness. It was the same question his father tried to answer, before he slapped him in his face, trying his best to ruin the face. But as the years went by and Giorgio was going from child to young adult, his face only got more striking.

It wasn't a façade that Larisa Rhodes was attractive to him. It wasn't a façade that anyone as wild and chirpy as Larisa was hooked on the aura of Giorgio Martel. Some of the Underground Devils saw it as a weakness, except for Larisa.

As for Giorgio, it didn't matter. Ever since he met Robin Jenkins, she was the only woman that Giorgio wanted to love. Death itself couldn't stop their love. From the first time they locked eyes, Robin became Giorgio's destiny. In Robin, Giorgio saw change. He saw the future. He saw a person that he could love inside and out. He thought to himself that he certainly wasn't going to find it in the Underground Devils.

Larisa walked back inside and sat next to Essence. The two together made a lethal connection. Larisa was a stripper in one of Dmitri's many clubs he acquired as well as an exhibitionist for pleasure before the Underground picked her up. Dmitri promised her sex and excitement if she worked for him. Being one of the youngest of the females to work for Dmitri, she found comfort in her new gang of friends, including Essence.

Larisa was known for getting any male she wanted. No one could resist her overwhelming passion, based off her training with the best masters in the art of seduction.

Unfortunately, Giorgio was a challenge for her. She wanted him every since he came from the street looking for a job, and just the fact that he was playing hard to get only increased her sexual fever. There was no being that could resist Larisa, and she ensured herself that Giorgio would not be the first.

Essence was not as attractive as Larisa. She was a mysterious she-devil with many secrets. One thing that wasn't a secret was her loyalty to Dmitri Sheppard and his beliefs. She would follow him to the ends of Greenwood if he ordered it. She became the model that Dmitri wanted all his soldiers to follow: undying loyalty. She did special jobs for Dmitri, taking out important people and potential enemies of the Underground. Larisa knew of rumors that said that Dmitri fathered a child of Essence that was sent to a special place for protection, but it had never been proven. Later on, it became one of several myths in the life of the Underground Devils.

"So what happen?" Essence asked as Larisa came back to her spot, pouting.

"Nothing," Larisa said.

"Nothing?"

Larisa folded her arms. "Something's going on with Giorgio. He's never acted like this before. You think he's hiding something?"

"Now what have I always told you about them? They always have secrets. Know all you can so you won't run into surprises."

"I think there's someone else."

Essence touched Larisa's face. "Who's more beautiful than you? Nobody! Get that shit out of your head."

"You think I should tell Dmitri?"

"Only if you need to. Be sure before you call out the heavy arms."

Larisa watched Giorgio come in from hiding. Dmitri saw him as well.

"Giorgio. My office," Dmitri said as he went back in. Giorgio followed Dmitri.

Cosine and Giorgio was in the office. It always scared him coming into the office. There was no telling what Dmitri did when the door was closed. While Giorgio was thinking about it, Dmitri presented him with pictures.

"This is your target."

Dmitri pointed to the face, an elderly man. "This is a priest whose church is in the way of our construction of one of our temples. His name is Father Aaron. I tried to make a reasonable bargain with him. Unfortunately, he wouldn't oblige. This is the test you have been looking for. Your job is to send this target to his maker. It may be a little edgy for you, but by doing this gets you a chance to take the next step. You gentlemen up to it?"

"Hell yeah!" Cosine said enthusiastically as he saw the picture."

Dmitri looked at Giorgio. "Giorgio?"

"I guess," Giorgio said, unsure of himself. He turned his head.

"You sure you're okay with this? Let me know if…"

"I'm fine."

Dmitri shrugged. "Trust me, I wouldn't let you guys do this if I didn't think you could handle it."

Cosine spoke for Giorgio. "You're given it to the right people, Lord Dmitri. Consider this done." He took the pictures and left, not thinking anymore about it. Giorgio slowly walked, but was stopped by Dmitri. Dmitri stared with eager eyes.

"Giorgio, you would tell me if something's wrong, would you?" Dmitri asked.

Giorgio tried his best not to look into Dmitri's eyes. His eyes were scary to him, like it was seeking deep into his soul.

"Of course," he said.

"You're still in this game, right? I'm going to need you more than ever. Our master needs you more than ever."

"Something tells me I really doubt that."

* * *

A man looked out from a window at the students of Sodom outside, walking, talking, among other things.

Ankaro Lindbergh loved what he did, being the high-ranking messenger to the Lord of Greenwood. He was considered the one who was manifested as the Lord, sending his prophetic messages to the masses. He had a very important job, a job that came with doing things that sometimes would create or destroy a life.

But Ankaro was a firm believer. He could handle those situations. He did it before and if the opportunity arrives that he had to do it again, it would not have to be asked twice.

Look at all those minds, he thought. *All those minds in search for a source.*

Ankaro walked around. His phone rang. Something in his mind knew who it was, but he answered it anyway.

"Hello! Oh, it's you. What do you want? Oh, you want to meet me tonight… How many times have I've heard that before? Where… Fine, I'll be there… Make sure you're there."

CARNAGE AND DISLIKE

COSINE SECANT WAS AN UNRULY TEENAGER WHO WAS KNOWN FOR turning his nose to authority. School, the streets, or anywhere he was, he was known to cause havoc. His brother Thorn Hawkins knew this, but tried not to say anything. Since they had no parents because their father died when Thorn was reaching his teens and Cosine was approaching five, they only had each other.

One thing Thorn did admire about his brother was that Cosine face the world better than he did. Even as a little boy, Cosine was not afraid and was ready to take risks. Before Thorn joined the side of the faithful completely, he had a little speed demon in him, but it didn't get as vicious as the path Cosine was taking. It had gotten worse since Cosine work on the side of the ruthless Dmitri Sheppard. He knew of the devil's reputation and mixed in with his devilish arts, Cosine would be a dangerous force.

Thorn was doing some work that night. He couldn't concentrate. For some reason, his mind was on the strange character known as Victor Marcus.

Where have I seen him from, he thought.

He found Cosine, rushing as fast as he could to the door.

"Cosine, wait!"

Cosine stopped. "What's going on, brother?"

"What's the rush?" Thorn asked.

"You know! Parties! That thing! You have to be there or you might miss something."

"Really?"

"Yeah!"

"This party doesn't have to do with Lord Dmitri Sheppard, does it?"

Cosine was shocked that he knew of Dmitri.

"What?" Thorn stressed. "That name doesn't ring a bell?"

Cosine shrugged. "How... How..."

"How did I know? Doesn't matter."

Cosine immediately thought of Vegas and how close he was to Thorn. "It was Vegas, was it? He don't even know what he's talking about."

"Dmitri's a dangerous character," Thorn said. "He can kill you with no hesitation or remorse."

Cosine was getting impatient. "I have nothing to do with Dmitri. Never had, never will. I'm just going to a party with some friends."

"Is that right?"

"That's it. That's all."

"Cosine, you know I care about you, right? I mean I only want to protect you."

"Sure."

"There isn't any 'sure.' I am. Be careful, okay? And don't be getting into trouble."

"Sure, Dad," Cosine said sarcastically.

"Better be lucky I'm not your dad because I definitely make sure you never go anywhere."

"Sure. I see ya."

Cosine rushed out the door, avoiding the last few minutes of the interrogation. This was common in the household, but Cosine visualized that he would have his own place soon and it would be the end of it. And that time was not long away. Following Dmitri Sheppard was going to make him wealthy beyond his wildest dreams.

* * *

Taking in a nice apartment from someone moving out was the dwelling place for Kim Silver and Erick Gold were two disciples working for the Grim Reaper. Working in the business as angels of death came naturally for the couple, but they took it to the next extreme, which didn't settle with their leader. Kim and Erick got a thrill out of killing priests, disregarding on whose side they were with. The lust for each other came afterwards, when the blood was cleaned from their bodies.

Erick and Kim did not remember their lives before they found the calling. That was one of the side effects of being a Reaper. The memories were lost forever unless needed or desired badly. Erick and Kim didn't want to know about their past. The way they saw it, why would they want to ruin a good thing. They held the power of death in their hands and no force in this world could stop it. What was even grander to them was that no one would even try. All they knew that whatever they did, it carried on to their lives. Erick and Kim liked to think that they were young lovers who died because they loved each other too much, and in a sense, it was the truth. They loved each other too much, and it caused pain and misery for others.

One thing they did remember was that they were together, going into death, and a Reaper came to them and asked them what they wanted out of the remaining life.

"I want to conquer death," Erick had said. "I want to love my love forever."

With that, their souls were taken and thus, they were on the way to becoming angels of death. They trained under the greatest of teachers, becoming the best students. And like in their past life, their love lingered.

"This is bull," said a pissed Erick as he swung his sophisticated knife around that carry his trademark skull. "Where can that damn child be?"

"It can't be farther from here," Kim said.

"It might as well be. I mean we look everywhere. We don't even know where or who the parents are."

"I'm sure all will fall in place when the child is found."

"I hope we find him soon. I do not want to keep dealing with the Black Reaper's bullshit."

"And we won't."

"As a matter of fact, I might as well call him. I'm sure he's going to want to know about this."

Erick picked up the phone and started to dial a number.

"Wait a minute!" Kim said as she took the phone from Erick and hung it up.

"What did you do that for?" Erick asked.

Kim paused for a few seconds and nodded her head.

"I just thought of something," she said.

"What?"

"Check this out. What... if we didn't tell him about the child?"

Erick took his time to think about it. "What are you saying?"

"I mean what if we didn't tell him about the child?" Kim asked again. "I mean when we find the child, let's not tell him where it is. Since we're doing the work and putting up with the bullshit, why should he get all the credit?"

Erick was confused. It made his head hurt when Kim came up with crazy schemes. Because he loved her too much, he never mentioned it.

"We don't even know where the child is," he said.

"Neither does he," Kim said. "And he's relying on us to find it. So why should we submit to this? I say we get something out of this."

"Like what?"

Kim stood up. "For one, the respect. And second, the title. We could become the Grim Reapers. Knock him out of the way and take it."

"Take it all? The child. The title. Everything?"

"Everything!"

Kim came close to Erick as he was getting excited.

"I like it, I like it, I like it," he said and brought Kim close to him by grabbing her buttocks. "You see, now I know why we work so well together? You know what I'm in the mood for?"

Erick hissed and Kim grinned at him.

"I'm in the mood to kill someone," he said. "Why don't we kill another priest tonight?"

Kim came to his face. "Baby, you have just read my mind."

"I love you, baby."

"I love you."

Erick and Kim shared a passionate kiss and much more.

* * *

A black car went down the street as fast as it could. As they drove off, another car parked near a church. Coming out of the car was four devils from Dmitri's crew, which included

Giorgio, Cosine, and Slash, the reliable and cold-blooded right-hand man of Dmitri. All four walked into a church. Sounds of screams and shattered glass were heard. They rushed out with two of them taking an injured priest with them. The priest was Father Aaron, their target. They put him into a car and drove off quickly. Suddenly, the church exploded and the fire started blazing as bright as it could.

* * *

A preacher got ready to close the church at night. He started walking out. He turned to face someone with a hooded cloak. Erick Gold took out the knife and stabbed him. Then, Kim Silver came out and stabbed him in the back. The preacher fell to the ground and the two killers stabbed him a few more times and disappeared into the shadows. But their love for killing knew no parallel. After the priest, Erick and Kim went on more killing sprees outside the Tri-Cities.

* * *

The four devils of Dmitri's crew walked in with the wounded Aaron. They threw him to the ground. Cosine and an unknown young devil started kicking and punching him. Giorgio stood there and watched, disgusted by the abuse. He could remember the last time that Cosine Secant was this ruthless. It was when he went to a man who was with his girlfriend after an afternoon to lunch. The man was probably in his late twenties, but it didn't fade Cosine one bit. He went to the guy and right in front of the woman, screaming to the top of her lungs, kicked him to the ground until he could barely stand.

Giorgio saw the heir to the Underground Devils Kingdom in Cosine.

Slash walked up in front of the rest of the devils.

"Alright, that's enough," he said. "Stand him up."

Cosine was the first to get Father Aaron up. Aaron staggered as he tried to stand. Slash took out his gun.

Slash said, "Well, here we are. You want to pray or something to your Lord before I start this? Because you're going to be praying to me soon enough."

Aaron remained resistant. "You can do what you want, but I'll never submit to you. The Lord will take care of the pain."

Slash smirked. Cosine looked at Aaron and smirked as well.

"Oh, he will?" Slash asked. "You really think so? You think your Lord cares about you? You're nothing to him, don't you understand? You could have belong to greatness, but you drown in pity for something that wishes you were dead anyway. I'm going to give you a chance. As a sign of good… faith!"

Aaron staggered to his feet. "You can take this body, but never my mind and soul. It belongs to…"

Before Aaron could say the rest, Cosine punched him to the ground. Slash looked over at a large wooden cross lying near him.

"I have an idea," Slash said. "Stand him up."

Cosine got Aaron up again. Slash took out his gun. The other devils stepped back. A shot ranged out from the gun. The bullet hit Aaron in the foot. Slash shot again and got the other foot. Aaron tried to grab his foot, but Slash quickly shot both of Aaron's hands. Slash shot multiple times in his chest and finally, to the head.

"Giorgio, get the cross," Slash ordered.

"What are you doing?" Giorgio asked, hoping this wasn't going to get out of hand.

"You'll see, kid."

Giorgio did what Slash said and gave him the wooden cross. With his massive size, Slash was too much for Giorgio. He knew better than to disobey him.

Slash said with a sinister voice, "We're going to hang him on the cross. Just like his master was. He'll be one of our messengers."

Cosine said excited. "That's creative,"

Giorgio turned his head. "That's sick."

"We're devils, Giorgio," Slash said. "We're supposed to be."

* * *

Looking down from a roof, Erick and Kim watched Dmitri's crew running out into the street. They took off their hoods.

"Well, look at this," Erick said. "Who are those guys?"

Kim looked closely. "Lord Dmitri's crew."

"And how do you know that?"

"I've seen them before. Club Lucifer. Dmitri's hideout. That's where all the young devils play."

Kim pointed to Slash.

"That's Slash, his right-hand man."

"You know," Erick said thinking ahead. "Something tells me they can be of use to us. We may not have to find the child. We can get them to find it for us."

"Does Dmitri even know about it?"

"He will soon enough. And with a few more murders, we can keep the agents busy so they won't get in our way."

Erick and Kim disappeared into the darkness once again.

* * *

Ankaro Lindbergh came inside a large mansion full of the color red in its decorations. Some females came to show him where he was supposed to go. They take him to a door, where there was large room. The females closed the door behind him. Ankaro saw, in the middle of the room, the person he wanted to see. From that point, he was getting uneasy.

It was the Marquis Red, the representative for the "Other Side," wearing his signature red and black to blend with his room. With a chessboard between them, Red folded his arms and stared at Ankaro. He could tell that he didn't want to be here. Red knew all about Ankaro as well as his master, and he played on that information.

Red and Ankaro were longtime opponents. One thing that paralleled them was their firm moments when it came to orders from their masters. Red became the spokesman for the devils, but in Ankaro's eyes, he was just a show-off, a playboy making himself feel better.

Ankaro sat down, with the chess table in front of him.

"Welcome!" Red said, pleased that he was not alone tonight. "I was expecting you sooner. But then again, when it comes to this, you were always right on time. Come! Play a game with me."

As he talked with the Marquis, Ankaro played chess, Red's favorite game. At one point, Red never knew why chess was such a great game, but after playing countless times and comparing the moves and strategies, he understood perfectly.

"I'm not in the mood for games," Ankaro said, trying his best to hold the anger in his veins.

"Of course you are," Red said, playing on the fear. "You're playing a game with me all the time."

"And what game is that?"

"The game of supremacy, of course. Your favorite game! And don't say it's not because it's my game as well."

"Really?"

Red was just getting started. "There's a difference, though. You're playing this game to prove your point. I'm doing it for the same reason… but also to get on your nerves. And from the look of it, I have done a good job. Look, I'm not a bad guy. Yet, you always treat me like I'm one. I just want the same thing you do. I want to win the game. You see what we're going through is just like this chess game. Why do you think I play it so much? It's war. With strategies, attacks and counterattacks. Isn't it lovely?"

"Yeah! Lovely!" Ankaro said sardonically. "I have to say you know this game. Since you want to talk about attacks and counterattacks, let's deal with one of your own. What is the deal with Dmitri?"

Red took a breath. It was a name that gave him grief.

"Dmitri Sheppard," he said. "A true disciple if it wasn't for his bloodthirstiness. He can lead armies, but he's not an administrator."

"He killed a priest. Peter Adams. And I'm sure he killed many others."

"I don't kill or send anyone to kill unless I have to. You of everyone should know that. You would have known anyway if I ordered anyone killed, beaten, or otherwise."

"I see."

Red made a few more moves on the board. He smiled at every move, which made Ankaro angrier than he ever was.

"Priest Adams," Red started again. "What makes you think Dmitri had something to do with it? Whoever did it was cunning. Dmitri is sloppy. Creative and inventive, but sloppy. And so is his crew. Follow him down to the very letter. But of course you would blame me for this. What about one of your own? They could have easily done this. Then again, he's a part of your army, so he couldn't be guilty. Never! It has to always be me. We're playing the same game. And let's face it! You'll do anything to win. This isn't really about some priest or some reckless youngsters. This is about our masters' huge egos. Too big for this world or many worlds. Oh, by the way…"

Marquis made his last move. "Checkmate!"

Ankaro stared at the board, then at the handsome face of Red. "Let's just say that Dmitri is not responsible. I'll be fine with whatever he does outside of the matter. However, if I find out, he will pay. I'll see to that."

Ankaro was disgusted. "I'll keep in touch."

"By the way!"

Ankaro stopped himself and took another dangerous look.

"However you may feel about me, let's get this one fact straight. Whatever goes on in this world, you'll always need me. Love me or hate me, you need me. Because I'll always be the one to make you look good for your children. Remember that."

Ankaro looked at the Marquis for a few seconds more and walked away, hoping never to come around his place nor see his face again.

WRONG MOVE

THE NEXT NIGHT, POLICE CARS WERE AT THE OLD, BURNED-DOWN church, observing the crime scene. Among them was the brave Shadow Fades. Shadow went to his captain, leading the scene, and walked with him to see the victim. Something told Shadow from the captain's look, he was as disgusted.

"This, I have to say, is the most gruesome thing I have ever seen," the captain said as he pointed overhead. "Take a good look at this."

Shadow saw the victim. It was Father Aaron, bloodied and hung above, nailed to a cross.

"More gruesome than the last two preachers," the captain said as he covered his mouth.

"The last two?"

"Not too far from here, another preacher was killed. It could be the same ones responsible."

Shadow observed the victim and the rest of his surroundings. "I don't think so."

"What are you saying?"

Shadow looked at his captain. "Whoever did this wanted people to know who they are. The other two murders were systematic. They wanted to keep it a secret."

Shadow saw something on the ground. It was a red slash.

"Dmitri!" Shadow said softly.

"Dmitri?"

"This was his gang's handiwork."

"Are you sure?"

"Who else?"

Shadow gave the slash to his captain and ran. All the captain could hear was burned rubber on pavement.

* * *

It wasn't as many people at Club Lucifer than it would have been, but it didn't bother Dmitri one bit. Since his club was the most happening place in the world, he didn't care if there was only one person in the club, mainly himself.

Shadow Fades stormed into the club, acknowledging this. Some of the guards tried to come in and stop him, but Shadow punched them around.

Shadow headed straight for Dmitri's office.

Within a few seconds, someone was thrown to the dance floor with a hard thump. It was Dmitri. Shadow ran to him as Dmitri tried to get up, knocking him down once again. The rest of his gang tried to get him, but Shadow took out his gun and waved it around. They could tell that his eyes were burning with rage. Then, he roughed Dmitri up by the collar and aimed the gun at his face.

"I knew it was you," Shadow said in his rage. "You cold-hearted bastard! You devils are all the same. By the grace of God I will kill you all if I ever see you around these streets again."

"I… I don't know…"

Shadow punched Dmitri, the hardest punch he threw in those few minutes.

"You know what I'm talking about," Shadow said as he slapped Dmitri twice. "You killed those three priests. And when I find all I need, I'll personally take care of you for good."

Shadow punched and kicked him a few more times before he got himself together and walked away. From the fast walk, he may not had gotten answers, but he was very liberated.

This was not typical for someone liked Shadow or his line of work or the criminals he faced. Around the time that Greenwood was just growing into a new peace, a police force was formed for the remaining demons and devils in the world that still wanted to raise chaos.

They were known as the Angel Guards and Shadow Fades was the best of them all. He didn't know about his past, and didn't care to know. All the doubts were erased when he accepted the Lord into his heart and soul.

Shadow went home to his secret hiding place and went on his knees. He held a cross in his hands. He usually said a prayer after his work was through for the day. Since he didn't have anyone to cry over, he usually never did.

"I must seek justice. Lord, give me the power to do so."

* * *

Math professor Dorian Ransom was finishing with his class lab at Sodom College. He was putting the rest of his books and things inside his backpack. As he packed up, another teacher came in: lifelong friend Gloria Burante.

The two could have shared a love affair according to others. Unfortunately, their two jobs, as teachers and faith practitioners for the Lord, kept the affair from going any further. Both care too much about their work to jeopardize their friendship. Dorian tried his best to keep his feelings inside. Gloria, however, was doing a good job with her emotions.

"Why do you always have to rush out of here like you can't stand this place?" Gloria asked with a smile.

"Hello, Gloria," Dorian said softly as if she was the last person he wanted to see. Gloria gave Dorian a friendly kiss on the cheek.

"I'm always like this," he said.

"Well, now you're about to have a purpose," Gloria said. "Cause I want you and me to have dinner at my place."

"You're asking me out?"

"You deserve it. You work so hard for these students, even though at times they don't know what you're saying and at other times don't care."

"Thanks for bringing up my confidence."

"Well, you can relax. I assure you."

Suddenly, a phone rang near them. Dorian answered it.

"Hello! Shadow, what's going on? Tonight? I don't have any plans. What's going on? Alright, fine, I meet you then. And I'll tell Gloria." He put the phone down.

"What's going on with Shadow?"

"I don't know. He said it was urgent."

* * *

Shadow stared off into the night. Walking to him was Gloria and Dorian, in their attire of white. They stood on both sides of him. Suddenly, wings came out from them, visible to Shadow and them and no one else.

Shadow was able to succeed in some of his cases thanks to the teachers. Dorian with his math skills, seeing things in a logical manner, and Gloria's way of detecting chemicals and pheromones, made the three a constructive force.

"This is nice," Dorian said.

"Very nice," Gloria agreed.

Shadow stared at them. "Glad you can make it."

"What is this about?" Gloria asked.

"I'm sure you have heard about the murders."

Dorian said, "The priests. Our boss told us."

Gloria said afterwards, "Apparently, it's a mysterious force at work here."

"It may not be that mysterious after all."

"What are you saying?" Gloria asked.

"The devils."

Dorian knew. "Dmitri and his gang."

"I think they have something to do with this. Don't worry! I gave him a message that he'll never forget."

Dorian and Gloria looked at each other.

"You didn't do that," Dorian said, shaking his head.

"Yes I did," Shadow bellowed. "It's too bad I didn't kill him when I had the chance."

Gloria was getting disappointed. "Do you know what you started?"

"Sorry to break it to you, but we are already in a holy war. It's been going on for decades."

"And you're making it worse for us," Gloria said. "We have to handle this the Lord's way and get to the bottom of this. This is his battle."

Dorian came to a decision. "We want you to back out for a while. Take a rest. We'll need you when the real danger comes. Dmitri's dangerous. We'll have someone else to handle him."

Shadow clinched his hands. "You want me to step back? You want me to give up my duty?"

Gloria knew that Shadow would get angry with this. She knew of his life. Gloria shook her head. "It's not like we are asking you to give up your duty."

"You might as well," Shadow said.

Dorian said sternly, "We'll need you later. When the real battle begins."

Shadow put his head down. "If this is what the Lord wants. It will be so. I will not interfere."

Gloria and Dorian walked away, leaving Shadow standing still.

I wish I can do that, Shadow thought, *but for once, I have to see this through.*

Shadow knew that the battles he fought would never end until he finished them. He figured at that moment that Gloria and Dorian knew what there was to him since they kept a close relationship.

* * *

This night was a special night for the Underground Devils. Every year they have a secret ceremony, the induction of new devils. This was the time in which after all the hard work, they would now become made devils. There were nine inductees for this particular ceremony, which included Giorgio Martel and Cosine Secant. While Cosine was thrilled, Giorgio felt more troubled that he ever was when he first joined the Underground. He thought about this as Slash was standing in front of them, staring at all the inductees. He knew that with this new phase in his time as a gang member, he knew that from this point on, things were going to get worse.

"You have proven yourself worthy to follow our master, the Prince of all Devils," Slash said in his majestic voice. "In standing here today, you are saying that you'll do whatever you have to do to follow you master… in life, in death, and in hell fire. With that in mind, you will now get you dark heart, our symbol. And as this burns, so may your burn and rot if you ever betray it."

The nine inductees took off their shirts and revealed their young, smooth backs. Each of the new devils got their black hearts, the tattoo to show that they were devils now and forever. With a large branding stick, they were given a mark of an actual black heart on their back. It was meant to be some sort of joke to the ones that experienced it, but it was meant all in honor. When the last one was branded, Dmitri entered. He smiled at the new nine inductees, no longer amateurs. They were now devil apprentices.

"Welcome," he said. "And enjoy the fruits of our labors."

The new devils got up and congratulated themselves. A big festival happened after that, with crazy music and seductive dancing. This was an usual time in which it was part-festival, part-business arrangement, in which Dmitri talked with his main officers about future plans.

In a nearby corner away from the party, Giorgio was calling on a phone to his lover, Robin.

"Robin. Hey, baby! Guess what? It's done. I'm a devil now."

Giorgio could tell that Robin was worried.

I don't know about this, she said. *I mean you know this is going to be more dangerous now. I mean what if they get you to kill someone?*

"I just won't do it."

And you think you can hold on to that?

"I'm not thinking about the dilemmas. I'm thinking about you and… Just know that we have to look out for each other because no one else will. Okay?"

If you say so.

"I love you."

I love you.

He put up his phone. He turned around and saw the lecherous Larisa standing there.

"Congratulations!" Larisa said with a smile that made Giorgio sick.

"Larisa!"

Giorgio knew that Larisa was attracted to him, but it was something in her that made him uneasy. Maybe it was the constant taunting of sexual attention she was letting off. Whatever it was, Giorgio wanted to get away from it. Too bad he wasn't as merciless as Cosine. He would have told it like it was and that would have been the end of it. He also knew of Larisa's reputation with her many admirers. She knew that this was all a game, and he refused every time she advanced. Still, she edged on. Giorgio knew from that moment that he was cursed.

"Yeah, it's me!' Larisa said. "Who else would it be?"

"What do you want?"

"What I want is what you got!"

Larisa went and kissed Giorgio. For a while, Giorgio accepted it, then backed away.

"I can't do this." Giorgio said.

Larisa was in heat and caressing Giorgio all over his chest.

"Oh, no!" Larisa said. "You're not going to do that again. There's no one else. Everybody's at the party. And I've been waiting for this for years. Ever since I laid eyes on you, I wanted you. I wanted your body. Your mind. Your soul. And now that you're one of us, there's no excuse why I can't take what's mine? You belong to me, just like you belong to Dmitri."

Larisa attempted to kiss him passionately again and Giorgio ran away. She walked back into the party.

I'll get you, Giorgio, Larisa thought. *And whoever you have on your shoulder will be yesterday's news.*

Essence entered, startling Larisa.

"Fail again I see?" she said.

Larisa was upset. Essence's presence only made it worse.

"I don't know what's going on," Larisa said. "Most of these guys will be all over me."

"Is that's why he's so special?" Essence asked. "The one you can't get?"

"Oh, I'll get him if it's the last thing I do. And I think I know a way."

"Well, for now, enjoy this party. There's some fresh meat out there, so you have a lot to choose from."

Essence and Larisa walked together back to the party. Essence was right. Larisa would forget about it for this night. Besides, she knew that she was the most beautiful creature in the world and she could have any male or female she wanted. Her body was the perfect pheromone.

* * *

Robin Jenkins was working on some papers while watching her baby boy. After hiding out with Giorgio in their love-nest apartment, she hid at her sister's place. Robin was an angelic innocent with a pure heart. She didn't believe in fighting unless the fighting was for something believable. For a time, she has been away from school and life entirely. All were centered on her child and her boyfriend.

She had known Giorgio for years since they met on the street. She was a high school student while he was an amateur criminal. To this day, she never knew what she saw in Giorgio, but she didn't regret it one bit, even when she had sex for the first time with him. Since then, they never left each other's side. Although, she worried about him, not only because he was working for Dmitri Sheppard of all people, but also if he stayed long enough, she was afraid that Giorgio would miss some of his old life as a devil and would want to return to it.

Larisa entered the door as Robin was getting something from the kitchen.

Robin Jenkins and Larisa Rhodes were sisters, but a lot of people, even Robin's close friends, could never tell how a guiltless soul like her had a demonically insane sister like Larisa.

Ever since they were little, they were more of rivals than sisters. When Robin came into the world, from that point on, there was a challenge without there officially being one. Larisa and Robin were competing for their mother's affection in intelligence, grace, and faith. Their mother was a demanding woman who wanted nothing but the best from her daughters.

When they were children, with their mother making ends meet just to support them, they wanted nothing more than to put a smile on their mother's face. Robin could do it, but Larisa was a hard case, always getting into trouble in the street. Larisa had the brawn and Robin had the brains. Larisa was the one the boys flirted with while Robin was always picked on for being a nerd.

When they became teenagers and Robin was developing her body, the roles reversed. Robin became the popular one while Larisa Rhodes nearly became a forgotten memory. Plus, Robin's intelligence was sharper, and Larisa was never a common sense person. As Robin was growing in popularity, so did Larisa's jealousy towards her. But she loved her mother, so she never took action toward her anger.

Then, Larisa joined the Underground Devils, and things were never the same. The respect for her mother diminished and she didn't need her self-respect because her mission in life now was to bring misery to her opponents through her body. She knew that was something Robin could never do because Robin was shy, an aspect that never escaped her. It didn't matter about the rejection with those closer to her. In Larisa's world, it was like they never matter.

But Robin was hiding out, and Larisa, like it was when they were little girls, was submitting to her younger sister.

"And what happen to you?" Robin asked as Larisa lounged in a chair.

"None of your business," Larisa answered, drunk and still feeling hurt by Giorgio's rejection. It seemed that because she was thinking about Giorgio the whole time, she couldn't enjoy the conquests she had gotten.

"Whatever," Robin said. "I really don't care."

"Of course you do," Larisa said. "What are sisters for, huh?"

"You? I don't know."

Larisa went to the baby, her nephew, and caressed his cute face.

"How cute he is," she commented.

Robin ran to her and slapped her hand.

"Don't touch him."

Robin went for a seat.

"What the big deal?" Larisa asked. "I can't touch my nephew?"

"You're no aunt to him."

Strict anger followed with Larisa. "Well, may I remind you that if it wasn't for me, you and his little ass would be out in the streets and you won't be able to enjoy the luxury we have now?"

Robin fired back. "After all I've done for you, it's the least you could do."

"Like what? With our mother? What the hell do I care about her? She don't mean a damn thing to me."

Robin got up and went to Larisa's face. "Don't you ever say that about our mother."

"Why? It's true. What, you're going to defend a whore? Go ahead. Defend her if you dare."

There was a pause. Larisa caressed Robin's face, making Robin ashamed for her. For the first time, Robin couldn't bare to look at Larisa. And the words she said about their mother confirmed everything.

"You're pretty just like her," Larisa said. "I use to be pretty like her until you came into this world. I have to wonder, though... would you... end up like her?"

Larisa passionately kissed Robin. Robin tried to push her away, but to no avail. Larisa moved back.

"You even have her lips," Larisa said. "Who would believe that?"

Larisa left slowly to another part of the house. Robin caught her breath, thinking the whole time could she ever hurt her sister, even if she was raised to create havoc. She wished someone would take her out of her misery. Or maybe... the misery lied in her.

A BABY

Shadow and a few agents went inside and raided one of Dmitri's businesses. It was a drug house, disguised as one of his smaller clubs. Since his last conversation with Dorian and Gloria, he carried out his own vigilante justice. He had it in his mind that Dmitri had something to do with the murder of the priests and he wasn't going to let it go.

"All of you are coming with me," Shadow said loudly to all the workers. "You resist, we shoot you dead. One of you is going to tell me where some of Dmitri's devils are."

Among the ones that watched him was Giorgio, who was talking with someone. He was stationed there to learn about the business. Shadow looked around until he saw Giorgio and vice versa.

"Giorgio Martel! Come on ahead down here."

With that, without thinking, Giorgio started running.

"Where the hell you going?" Shadow roared.

A chase commenced between Giorgio and Shadow. Other people got in the way of Shadow and were knocked down by the other agents. Giorgio was going down streets until he reached an alley and stopped. He was trying to catch his breath.

"What the hell is he doing?" Giorgio said. "I don't need this."

Suddenly, Shadow came from behind and hit Giorgio in the back. Giorgio fell to the ground. Shadow then put his hands behind his back and placed the handcuffs on him.

"The Lord says that you're under arrest," Shadow said relieved.

"What did I do?"

"It's not what you did. It's what you're going to do. Get up." Shadow roughly raised Giorgio up. "Time to take a little trip."

Shadow took Giorgio up to an unknown black river. He went to the other side of his car and let out Giorgio, still in handcuffs. Shadow took them off and pushed Giorgio.

"What is this all about?" Giorgio asked, thinking of a way to get out of this.

"Needed a quiet place to talk," Shadow said.

"About?"

"Your boss. I heard you got in a few nights ago."

"And who told you that?"

"Some birds told me," Shadow said ironically. "It's surprising what you can get from them. They can see inside things we can't."

"So what?"

Shadow's anger started to rise.

"Okay, kid, let's get the real deal," Shadow said. "You have something I want and you will do it for me. I want your boss."

"I will?" Giorgio said. "And what makes you think that?"

Shadow calmed down, while inside, he was ready to knock some sense into Giorgio. "Because I know that you're not like Dmitri or any of his gang."

"What makes you think I can't kill you right here and now?"

Shadow chuckled. "Go ahead if you can."

Giorgio tried to hit him, but stopped himself.

"You don't have the killer in you like Dmitri," Shadow said, not moving a spot. "Help me take him down, Martel."

"Even if I wanted to, what makes you think I'll do that? I will not get killed for you. Understand?"

Giorgio took a few steps away.

"Whatever you're trying to hide," Shadow said, "you won't be able to hide it for long. Soon, you're going to need my help."

Shadow turned around and headed for his car.

"I don't need shit from you," Giorgio said angrily. "And if you do this again, I'll…"

Shadow turned his head. "What?"

"DAMN!."

Giorgio screamed in frustration, knowing if he would fight Shadow, he would lose miserably, and just walked away.

"You don't want a ride?" Shadow asked, trying his best to be considerate.

"I can walk. I'm used to it now."

Shadow watched Giorgio walked away, thinking that he had made a small, but good leap in the right direction.

* * *

Cosine sat with Dmitri in one of Club Lucifer's secret rooms that day, along the rest of the gang, including Slash and Essence.

"That cop is raiding all of the businesses," Slash said. "Who the hell does he think he is?"

"He's respected around the town," Dmitri proclaimed. "Going up against him is like going up against God himself."

Essence jumped up. "Respect? He beat you up in front of people in your own club and you're giving him respect?"

Dmitri still felt the pain from that night, rubbing the black bruise that appeared on his face, and he didn't want to relive it. He snapped his neck to get it flexed and stared at Essence.

"He said I killed three priests," Dmitri said. "Slash, what did you guys do that night?"

Slash answered, "We only went after the priest you wanted us to, which I must say is some of my favorite work."

"Then it's someone else trying to cut in."

"What are you going to do?" Slash asked.

"Well, first, I'm going to find out about those other two priests…"

"And Shadow?" Cosine asked, anxious to kill since his elevation in rank.

"We'll see about that. Look, I have to be alone for a while. So, if there's anything else, go away."

Dmitri walked away. He went down to his office, staring at a twisted painting, his description of planet Greenwood. Or the way he wanted it to be. It was his inspiration to continue doing what he did, and to never forget who the enemy was.

His phone suddenly rang and he picked it up.

"What?"

The voice was dark and sinister. *Dmitri Sheppard!*

"Who is this?"

Someone who is a big fan of your work. I have to say, you did a… creative job on that priest. I couldn't have done it better with the other two that I've killed.

"You killed the other two priests?"

We want to talk business. Your expertise is very much needed. You and you alone.

"Name the place."

Minutes later, before he knew it, Dmitri looked out into the night, standing on top of a roof, thinking of who in the world knew where he was, as well as wondering if this trip was worth it.

"Why am I doing this?" Dmitri asked himself. "I'm Lord Dmitri, dammit!"

Dmitri turned around and saw three Reapers with their signature black cloaks on. All three took off their hoods. It was Erick, Kim, and another secret reaper, Platinum, who works as an assassin.

"Did you think you would wait long," Eric said in his sweet voice.

Dmitri sneered. "Reapers. I should have known. It makes sense now. I thought you all were just myths."

"Well, now that we got that out the way," Kim said, "let's get down to business."

"Which is?"

Erick started it off. "We need you and your gang's help in finding someone for us."

"A baby," Kim said, cutting him off.

Dmitri chuckled. "A baby! Are you kidding? You must be. A baby? You brought me all the way up here to discuss a baby?"

"This isn't an ordinary baby. A baby born from an angel and a devil. The perfect harbinger."

Erick said, "An incrimination to anything and everything. From the order to the chaos, which is the only thing that can come out of all this."

"It's that much of a threat?" Dmitri asked.

Kim said, "If this child grows up, it will have the power to destroy angels and devils alike. We have come here to find the child and claim it, but it seems that we're out of luck."

Erick stuck out his hand. "And that's where you come in. You and your gang can go to some of these places freely like we can."

"You're Reapers. And you can't do it?" Dmitri folded his arms.

Erick said, "Like you, we have superiors. And there's serious when it comes to ethics. You can be free, even if your master doesn't want you to."

"Okay, let's just say that I do this for you. What's in it for me? This doesn't come free."

Erick touched his chin with his finger. "Well… we heard that you have some… adversaries that you need to get rid of."

Kim looked at Eric and then at Dmitri. "Does a name Shadow Fears ring a bell?"

"Heard he made an embarrassment out of you in your establishment and it's eating you up inside," Erick said.

Dmitri couldn't believe that they knew Shadow. On top of that, they were making fun of him about it.

"What makes you think I care about Shadow?" Dmitri asked.

Kim said, "We also know he and other agents are raiding your businesses, scaring your soldiers."

Erick made a graceful gesture with his hand. "We can get rid of that interference for you."

Dmitri had to get somewhere with them. "What makes you think I can't take care of him myself?"

"Because if you do," Kim said, "you have all sides going against you. However, we do it, no one will expect and your hands will be clean."

Erick came in. "We can take care of him and all other problems for you. All we ask is find the child and their parents and bring them to us."

"All my adversaries?" Dmitri asked.

Kim went to Platinum. "Platinum," she said, "have you met Lord Dmitri Sheppard of the Underground Devils Gang? Dmitri, this is our apprentice, Platinum." Kim caressed Platinum's face with her own. "She'll take care of your agent friend, won't you, darling?"

Platinum, who usually didn't said much, told Kim in her secret language, "Anything for you, my master." Then, she kissed Kim on the mouth, which sort of disgusted Dmitri, but enticed Erick.

"See?" Erick said. "Nothing but trust here! What do you say, Dmitri?"

"This might be nice," Dmitri said. "Fine, I'll find your little brat."

Kim gave him a warning. "Know this. If you don't keep your word, then we'll pay you a visit that comes with no words."

"Other than that," Erick said, "consider the problem solved."

"We'll see you around."

The three Reapers walked away, side by side. Dmitri knew he was getting in over his head, working with Reapers, the most vicious negotiators. And he thought that Vegas Armano was a headache. And what about this baby bore from an angel and a devil? Who would possibly be in love with each other to produce a child? Dmitri knew he had to find answers.

* * *

Since Thorn Hawkins won the Tri-Cities Collegiate Title from Roberto Ruiz, he had just won his third defense of the title. A gladiator through and through, he toughed it out and managed to win another fight, thus increasing the positive legend that was growing around him. During the fight, Thorn looked at three people: Cecilia, Vegas, and the mysterious Victor, who stared cold at Thorn for some odd reason. Somehow, he was thinking to himself that there could be a connection between the three. *An outlandish connection.*

After the game, Thorn and Cecilia walked on to Thorn's car. Suddenly, Vegas came to them.

"Hey, lovebirds," Vegas said cheerfully.

"What's going on?" Cecilia asked. "Why you guys going so soon? I thought we could go to the club or something?"

"I'm down with that."

Thorn shook his head. "Not me, thanks! I'm just going to go home."

Vegas touched Thorn's shoulder roughly. "Come on, man! When the last time you had any fun?"

"I just did."

"I'm talking about outside the ring?"

Cecilia went to Thorn's other shoulder. "Come on, baby. I let you do things to me!" She went and licked his ear, making Thorn shiver a little.

"I guess…" Thorn looked into his bag. "Ah! I forgot something in the locker room. I tell you what, I'll just meet you guys there."

"You better," Vegas said "or I'm taking your girl home tonight. My home, that is."

"Don't even think about that."

Thorn ran away while Vegas and Cecilia watched.

Vegas changed the subject. "Oh, guess what? I got the perfect present for Robin."

"Do you think this is good?" Cecilia asked. "I mean, with those guys chasing her and all."

"Does Thorn know?"

"Of course not."

"Good. Knowing him, I don't think he would handle this well. He and Robin are close. Almost like brother and sister."

"He won't know. Don't worry."

Vegas and Cecilia walked on. Unknown to them, Victor and a large man, nearly the size of all three friends he was spying on combined. He looked as Thorn went back inside a building as well as Vegas and Cecilia, who was playing around with each other, or at least Cecilia was getting Vegas to stop. Then, they look at each other and the large man walked away, heading the same direction Thorn was going.

* * *

Thorn was the only person in the locker room. It was too quiet for Thorn and it made him anxious. He was getting the reminder of his things when he heard noises. He circled around. Then, he started walking slowly. He took one more step and then, was punched against the locker by an unknown hand.

Thorn looked at his puncher. It was the large, muscular bodyguard standing next to Victor Marcus. The henchman fought as if he was a street fighter while Thorn only had his football skills to defend himself. He practiced boxing, but this was different. This henchman has been around and fought many battles as far as he was concerned. Knowing himself, he rose to the challenge. At first, the large man had the upper hand, but Thorn fought back, and with his punches working faster into the henchman's chest, he was able to weaken the large man to the floor. He hit him with an uppercut that nearly killed him. Thorn caught his breath, got what he came for, and ran away. When he left, the henchman raised himself, wiping his breastplate away of the pain he almost felt. He thought to himself had Thorn Hawkins kept going, he probably wouldn't have a chance.

* * *

Shadow was resting on the floor of his secret hideout, looking at the ceiling with little light in the shack. He knew that what he was doing was a big mistake and that Dmitri would go after them, but that was the least of his problems.

Suddenly, he noticed something unfamiliar. His shadow was moving. His shadow, which was standing still as he was staring at it, was moving bit-by-bit.

That's odd. Why is my shadow moving like that?

Suddenly, the shadow disappeared completely, which made Shadow rise from the floor. Then, flying through the air came a person with a black cloak. It knocked Shadow to the ground. The cloak person stood on a table, eying Shadow. Shadow could see the skull over her face used as a camouflage. The person took off the hood and the skull. Shadow immediately stood up.

"Did Dmitri send you?" he asked.

"Hardly," the assailant said in her dark voice.

He launched to Shadow with mist and threw it into his eyes. Shadow struggled to shake it off, but then he started attacking him from all sides and lighting speed. When he was about to regain his eyesight, he was stabbed in the back with the assassin's sword. He fell to the ground. Then, the supernatural figure destroyed the place, starting from the roof, quickly leaving the place before the whole house collapsed with Shadow Fades in it.

* * *

Dmitri sat in his office and heard his phone ring. He picked it up. It was Platinum.

"Yes!"

Lord Dmitri Sheppard! The deed has been done. Shadow Fears has been… faded. Now that your problem is done, handle ours.

The phone hanged up on the other line. Dmitri slowly hanged his phone up. Another adversary of Dmitri out of the way. Now, Dmitri was more relaxed than tense from before when he met the Reapers.

* * *

People were dancing and drinking wildly at another crazy club known as the X-Club as others make their presence known with their stylish clothes. Unlike Club Lucifer, the X-Club was classier.

Thorn came in, trying to get himself together. He was feeling pain from those hard punches, thanks to the henchman. Vegas and Cecilia walked to him.

"What took you so long?" Cecilia screamed.

Vegas said, "Trying to escape the deal. I knew it."

Thorn looked at another direction. "Vegas, I need to talk to you in private. Cecilia, I'll be right back."

Thorn and Vegas walked to a corner, trying to get people out of their way.

"Now what is up with you?" Vegas asked, ready to party.

Thorn was stressed. "Someone try to kill me."

"What?"

"Someone tried to kill me! Some large dude."

"Who?"

"I don't know. I think I killed him."

"Are you sure?"

"What do you mean am I sure?"

Vegas touched Thorn's chest lightly. "Okay, look! If you want to, we'll go back and see. And if he's dead, then we'll have to find some possible solution."

"There's something else. I think I saw this guy before. He was with… he was with Victor Marcus."

"That crazy bastard?"

"He was with him when we first saw him. I didn't mind it then, but then I saw him at the game sitting with him."

"What for?"

"I don't know. But I don't think I killed him. I just stunned him."

Vegas was relieved. He was not about to ruin this night on the count of Victor Marcus. "Well, good! Because we're going to have fun tonight and nothing's going to ruin it, especially not his ass. So let's go to our table, you say hello, cuddle up with your girl before I do, and we'll discuss this in the morning. So enough about this."

Vegas put his arm around Thorn and both walked to their table. Cecilia greeted Thorn with a hug and a kiss on the cheek.

"You men got whatever you got out of your systems?" she asked.

"We're good," Vegas said.

Cecilia looked to Thorn. "Well, I'm in the mood to dance. You up for it?"

Thorn sat down. "I need to think about something."

"Well, I wanna dance," Vegas said. "Don't worry! I'll keep my hands to myself."

Vegas took Cecilia's hand and they went to the dance floor. Thorn looked around for Victor's henchman, thinking about what another beating would do. He saw Vegas and Cecilia, laughing up a storm as they embarrassed themselves on the dance floor. In a sense, it made him smile.

Then, someone caught Thorn's eye. It was an entourage of people. Thorn stood up when he recognized one of their faces. He saw Giorgio, and the rest of Dmitri's gang, wearing nice, stylish suits.

"I know that's not Cosine."

Thorn walked to them. Without words, he took his brother's arm and walked him back to the door, despite others coming in and taunts by his gang and Cosine.

Outside the X-Club, Cosine and Thorn went near an alley. Thorn roughed him up by his collar.

"What the hell is your problem?" Thorn shouted in anger. "What are you doing here?"

Now Cosine was enraged. "What is wrong with you, man? Trying to embarrass me in front of my friends?"

"And didn't I tell you about Dmitri?"

"Yeah, yeah…"

Thorn roughed Cosine up again, bellowing, "Listen to me. This ends, you understand? This ends now!"

"What are you, my father? You don't run me."

"As long as you under my roof, you obey me."

"Well, that's gonna change! So if you don't mind, I'm going back to my friends."

Thorn grabbed his arm, but Cosine pushed him. Thorn heard Cosine growling under his breath.

"Don't cross me, Thorn," he said. "Don't you dare cross me."

Cosine strolled away as Thorn tried to get himself together. He remembered Cosine mentioned their father. If their father was still alive, he would die a thousand deaths in seeing at what Cosine had become. He walked back to the party, trying to piece what he was going through within a few hours of his good time. First, a stranger tried to kill him, and now, his brother has found a new breed of defiance. He was about to reached for the entrance to the X-Club, but then, he turned away and headed for his car to go home.

FAREWELL, LITTLE BROTHER

LATELY, THORN COULDN'T CONCENTRATE ON HIS WORK BECAUSE OF THE nights he had: the fight with Victor's henchman left him bruised, his relationship with his brother was on the downslide, and Cecilia's constant wants and needs for his attention were increasing, and getting on his nerves. Even with the teacher talking, it sounded like gibberish. He continued to look serious but inattentive. He knew that no class was going to cure his inner pain.

Thorn walked to his car. As he did, Cecilia ran to him with exhilarating excitement. Thorn continued to walk. He didn't want to hear her.

"Thorn! Thorn, stop!"

Thorn stopped to look at her. Cecilia saw from his face that something was bothering him and she knew what that might be.

"What you want?" Thorn asked abruptly.

"What's wrong with you?" Cecilia asked.

"I don't mean to say this, but I can't talk with you right now. As a matter of fact, it'll probably be a while before I say anything to you."

"Because of your brother? I heard what happened. What did he do to make you act this way?"

Cecilia could read him like a book. The last thing he needed from her was her help, especially with his energetic brother.

"It's a lot of things," Thorn said. "It doesn't matter."

Thorn was rubbing his head. The, he came out with it.

"Look, I think we just need some time apart, okay?"

Cecilia was silent for a few seconds. She hoped it wasn't what she thought she heard.

"You don't mean that?" she said as miniature tears formed.

Thorn was disappointed, but he always stuck with his decisions, his blessing and his curse. "I just don't need you around me, alright? Don't make this any harder for me as it is."

Cecilia was silent again. Then, she said, "If… that what you want… I'll just… see you around."

"Yeah!"

Thorn walked on to his car without another word or another glance. Cecilia looked at him for a few seconds, then turned around and walked in the other direction. She had lost her beau to his own brother. It was not from a love affair from another woman. In the end, she thought of what she knew all along. Duty came first in Thorn's life, and Cecilia sensed the signs. Now, Thorn was gone and she was alone. As she walked, not believing the turn of events, she could had sworn that she saw Victor Marcus staring at her with the most detrimental eyes. But looking from the distance was Victor Marcus, with his large henchman, smiling at the event as if it was his victory. Cecilia made an obscene gesture and walked forward.

At his home, Thorn sat down at a table, thinking about what he was doing and what would it accomplished. He had homework, but his mind wasn't focused enough to do it. Was everything he was doing going to get his brother back, he didn't know. As he was thinking about his brother, his phone rang. He picked it up.

"Hello!"

Is this Thorn Hawkins?

"Who wants to know?"

We called to talk to you about Cosine Secant? Apparently, he has not been coming to school in weeks and we hoped there are no problems.

"I didn't… There are no problems."

If there's any problem-

"I will called you."

Cosine is a good student.

"Yes he is!"

Thorn hung up the phone quickly, reached for his jacket, and headed out the door.

* * *

At Club Lucifer, lounging in a chair like he was a king, Dmitri talked with Essence, Larisa, and Slash in a secret room. Since his club was large, he had many secret rooms, whether he needed to hold special meetings with his main officers or he needed to hide things from the outside world.

"We have a change in our plans," Dmitri said. "Something has come up."

"What about Shadow Fades?" Slash asked.

"Shadow Fades is no longer a problem for us."

"Too bad. And I wanted the pleasure of rearranging his face for what he did."

"Don't worry, Slash. There's plenty of time for that."

Essence stood up. "So what are these plans?"

"We have been asked to do a special favor," Dmitri told Essence. "We have been asked to find someone."

Larisa asked. "Who? An enemy of ours?"

"An innocent bystander," Dmitri said. "A baby."

"A baby?" Larisa shrieked. "Is that what this is all about? A baby?"

"Apparently, this is no ordinary baby," Dmitri said cheerfully. "This is some child born from an angel and a devil. A child who if it grows up, can have enough power to destroy this world." A boisterous chuckle came from his mouth and everyone laughed with him. "Unfortunately, we don't know where the baby is or who the parents are."

"So that's where we come in?" Essence asked.

"This is perfect for our new recruits. Slash, I want you to lead them. Search all over these towns within the Tri-Cities and find this child. Terrorize whoever and whatever you need to. Bring the babies you find here and we'll see who the spawn is."

"And how would we know who it is?" Slash asked.

Dmitri took out a medallion and put it around his neck. "This will tell us," he said as he showed his comrades. "A gift from our special visitors. This is a spawn medallion. When babies of this magnitude are born, then a mark is branded on them. It's whether the branded mark lights up that show the spawn. And if they are right about this, then this baby's mark, when we put it on, will shine a light so bright, no angel or devil can withstand it."

Dmitri heard some noise, the sounds of fighting and anger. Larisa heard it too.

Dmitri noticed something. "That voice."

He got up and left the room. The rest of the gang followed him. When the gang got there, they saw a large fight going on between devils of his gang and a vengeful Thorn Hawkins.

"Stop!" Dmitri commanded.

The gang backed away from Thorn. Dmitri stood topside as Thorn was looking at him from below. For the time he remembered knowing him, Dmitri respected Thorn, for what, he didn't know. Maybe it was because he was to his Lord what he was to the Prince of Devils: a dutiful servant.

"Well, well, well," Dmitri said as he raised his arms in the air so all would see him. "If it isn't the champion Thorn Hawkins. Sodom's best! What's going on, man?"

"Dmitri!" Thorn said under his throat, holding his rage.

"This is a surprise. A big surprise."

"Like I care."

Dmitri grinned. "Okay! So you want to cut to the chase, fine. What do you want?"

"My brother," Thorn said. "Cosine Secant. I want him back. You're not going to fool him like you fool all these people."

Dmitri was surprised. "Wait a second! Cosine is your brother? I have to admit, he doesn't look anything like you."

He and the gang started laughing, but this only made Thorn's adrenaline intensify.

"I don't have time to joke with you," Thorn shouted. "You haven't change since we were little. You're worse than you was before."

"I don't have time to go down Memory Lane with you."

"Then get me what I want."

Slash was livid. "You son of a bitch. Who do you think you are?"

Slash was about to attack, but Dmitri put his arm out to stop him.

"Bring Cosine here," Dmitri ordered.

"But Lord Dmitri…"

"Do it!"

Slash went to get Cosine.

"We'll let him decide," Dmitri said to Thorn. "And it'll solve everything."

"I hate you," Thorn said. "I hate you for what you're doing to my brother."

"Aren't you forgetting something? You can't hate. Your master won't let you. It's a weakness."

Dmitri smiled at Thorn for bringing him back to reality. As this happened Cosine and the rest of the gang came down, including Giorgio, who was just curious.

Dmitri looked at Cosine. "Well, here he is. Cosine, come to me. Looks who's here to see you."

Cosine came and stood next to Dmitri like they were father and son.

"Cosine, listen to me," Thorn said. "I know you don't want this. Why don't you come with me? I forgive you for your anger. I want to take you home."

This was the moment Dmitri was waiting for. A sure-fire debate with the Greenwood God's future champion.

"And what are you going to do, Thorn?" he asked. "Let me guess. You're going to take him home. You going to teach him those things that was told to you, about ethics and honor or whatever. Fill his heads with a bunch of lies."

"You're feeding him lies."

"I'm giving him truth. As much as I can say for you and those angels you follow. Him going with you will make him miserable, just like you." He turned to Cosine. "Cosine, what do you want? Do you want to follow your brother, go out and follow the laws of a master who doesn't cares about you and have you living in a box. Or do you want to stay with me and be free. Do whatever you want. Be whatever you want."

"He's lying to you, Cosine," Thorn blurted. "He doesn't care about you. You're just an asset to him. A means to an end. You mean nothing to him."

Thorn was rubbing his throat, trying to think of the rest of the words. "Look, you're still my brother no matter how much we fight or argue. I still care about you. I will still fight for you. Let just go home and start this over." He stuck out his hand. "Just take my hand. Let's go home."

Cosine looked at Dmitri and then at Thorn. Cosine slowly started walking down the stairs and to Thorn. He took out his hand. Thorn grabbed it and hugged him. Dmitri and the gang stood their ground.

"I love you, brother," Thorn said. "I forgive you for getting mad."

Suddenly, Thorn felt a pain to his chest. He stepped back. To his shock, he found out that his little brother Cosine, with his little fingers, stunned him in his chest like they were knives. Thorn was shocked. Where did his brother get his power? The pain was killing him.

"You may have forgiven me," Cosine said with a threatening smile, "but I haven't forgiven you."

Cosine used an energy blast from his fingers and carried Thorn back to the wall and to the floor. The gang went to Cosine and patted him on the back. Thorn's Sodom jacket was torn. He looked like a battered boxer, trying to stay alive.

An amused Dmitri walked to a wounded Thorn. "Well, it looks like I'm his brother now. But don't worry! I won't make the same mistake you did."

Thorn was trying to get up, reaching for Dmitri's feet. He staggered to his feet.

"I'm going to get you, Dmitri," he said under his breath. "You understand me? You're going to die!"

Dmitri started laughing. "You and what army? Get him out of here."

Some of Dmitri's devils picked him up and threw him outside. All of the gang walked away except Giorgio, who watched Thorn being taken out and Cosine's amusement. This could have been an alley for Giorgio to escape the prison he has placed himself. Seeing Cosine enjoyed the fruits of being a devil made his nauseous.

Thorn was thrown to the street by Dmitri's gang, after a few more punches and kicks. He got up slowly, looked at the club, gave out some taunts, and walked away from it, holding his belly. Looking from above the club's roof was Victor Marcus, shaking his head as Thorn walked alone, not accomplishing what he was set out to do.

Thorn.

As Victor stared, in entered his henchman, standing to his side.

"Look at him," Victor said. "A charming fellow turned to rubbish. Well, rest assured, Thorn Hawkins, your luck will change soon enough."

A pause.

"The plans have been set. Thorn has broken up with Cecilia. His brother is at the hands of his enemy. He wants war. And he'll get it."

Victor turned to his henchman. "Are you ready?"

The henchman nodded.

"Good, because we'll soon have a fight on our hands."

The henchmen nodded again.

"By the way, I must give a message to a fellow friend of mine. Ask him to continue to monitor the skies. Make sure our friends haven't made any steps ahead of us."

Victor Marcus walked away from his henchman. A plan was forming. For now on, if only in his mind, Victor Marcus would hold the keys to Thorn Hawkins's fate.

THE LOVE-AND-WAR AFFAIR

SHADOW WOKE UP IN AN EXQUISITE BEDROOM, WITH BANDAGES ON him. After fighting an unknown phantom and having his whole hiding place fall in front of him, he thought he was dead for sure. Something told him the anger he felt at losing the battle or any battle for that matter was probably the only thing that kept him alive. He got up and looked around, feeling the pain with each stretch.

"Where the hell am I?"

Dorian Ransom entered.

"You're up," he said. "Finally. Thought we lost you for a minute there." He turned his head. "Gloria, he's up."

Gloria entered right behind him with some food.

"Good," she said. "Here, eat something."

Shadow looked around the room as he was presented food from Gloria. For teachers, how were they able to live in a palace of gold and silver, he wondered.

Gloria said. "You would've been dead if we didn't find you in time. What happened?"

Shadow was getting edgy. "Someone attacked me. I don't know who, though. They blinded me with some mist. All I know is this person was fast and knew how to fight."

"Who do you think it is?" Dorian asked.

"No doubt about it," Shadow said. "It was someone from Dmitri's gang."

Dorian was livid. "We told you to don't go further with this."

"And for a time I didn't. Now, Dmitri has made this personal. And I'm going to kill him."

"Sorry to disappoint you," Gloria said, "but we think that this has nothing to do with Lord Dmitri or your attacker, or even the priests that were murdered."

"What are you saying? There's something else to this?"

* * *

Vegas went into a restaurant. Despite Vegas loving and thriving on attention, he had quieter moments. There were some moments he wanted to get his head together and his mind went to the past. So far, his future was looking bright. He was able to get anything he wanted in the world and beyond that, he was an rebel angel with special powers.

Going to a nearby bar, he wanted to get a good snack before he went back home. He looked around and saw his friend, Cecilia, by herself, without Thorn. This was strange. Cecilia never went anywhere unless Thorn or he and Vegas were with her.

This time, she was alone, and in her peculiar way, drowning her sorrows in wine.

This was not one of her usual moods, Vegas noticed. The cheerful Cecilia was not a moping presence. This made him unusually curious. He went and sat down on the other side of her.

"Want company?" he asked.

"Like that'll stop you anyway," Cecilia said.

"What's wrong? Don't look like your cheerful self. Where's Thorn?"

"Don't know and don't care."

Vegas knew something happen. He didn't know whether to be mad at her or Thorn.

"That's not like you," he said.

"Yeah, well, this isn't one of my normal moods," Cecilia said as she put her hand on her chin.

"What's going on?"

Cecilia answered, "Just what I need. Being pimped by an angel."

But he is a cute one, she thought. Cecilia couldn't shake that meticulous feeling off about him. Vegas had the aura around the sector of his well-being.

"Thorn broke it off with me, okay?" Cecilia screeched and put her head down.

This intrigued Vegas.

"Over what?" he asked. "What did you do this time?"

"And what make you think it's me?"

"Well, I have to say, you didn't have the greatest reputation."

"Look, I made mistakes," Cecilia said, holding on to Vegas' hand. "Everyone does. Thorn just wanted to break it off. I think it's his brother."

"Well, I tell you what. You come with me to discuss some business with Robin tonight and then, we'll paint the town red. What you say?"

"I don't know."

"Well, you need to cheer up. And if you don't want to do it with me, then with someone."

She didn't know what kind of a game Vegas Armano was playing, but being who he was, she loved it anyway. For a brief second, she was thinking did she choose the wrong guy to love?

* * *

The Reapers Erick and Kim were having sex. This went on for a few minutes until they reached their peaks. A mixture of lust and death was in the air and they love every particle of it.

They stopped, caught their breaths, then relax in a split second. As agents of death, they knew how to regain power easily and never tired. Kim went on top of him.

"You're the best as usual," Erick said.

Kim kissed him. "Thank you."

"I must say. Getting Dmitri to do this for us was a good idea. This way, we'll be able to relax."

Kim got up and turned around. Erick saw a distraught look in Kim.

"What's wrong, darling?" Erick asked.

"I… I was thinking," Kim said. "How well can we trust Dmitri?"

"You suggested we use him and now you're not so sure we can trust him."

"No, it's not that. It's something else."

Kim touched her head. "Do you remember when the lieutenant talked to us about the baby? He said something I'm just now thinking about. About the baby's power."

"Yeah, and if it's grow up, it'll be destructive," Erick said. "Yeah, I know that."

"Not that."

A pause.

"He said that whoever possesses the child could possess the power," Kim said, "… like a sort of from being a mentor to him or something like that."

"Wait," Erick said. "You're saying that if we find the child, then we could become powerful?"

"I guess so! And to think that didn't come up to my head before, and we're letting Dmitri find him for us. What if he knows that, too?"

Erick threw an object against the wall and slapped Kim across the face.

"Are you crazy?" Erick asked furiously. "What do you think he'll do?" He rushed out of the bed. "Get up. We got to find that child before he finds out what kind of power it holds."

Erick and Kim got up and left the apartment in a hurry.

* * *

Dmitri was reading a book as loud head-banging music was playing at his club. He saw something that caught his eye.

Dmitri was reading. A phrase stuck in his mind. "…Behold you give me a devil of creation and I'll give you an angel of destruction…"

Then came the thoughts. *Angel of destruction? A child born from an angel and a devil that possesses both entities… The possessor of the child can… possess its power and become its master. Could this be the child the Reapers were talking about?*

Dmitri closed the book slowly and grinned. Then, he heard the sound of babies crying. Dmitri's gang went all over the Tri-Cities and other towns within the past few days and found over five hundred babies. So far, he found no one with the secret power. But in hearing this, a new thought process was in order in Dmitri's mind. He didn't need the Reapers, and if he found the child and the truth lied with the words, he wouldn't even need his Underground.

* * *

Robin opened the door to her place. It was Vegas and Cecilia. She gave both of them a hug. She was always happy to see these two. They, along with Thorn Hawkins, who was like an older brother, were the only people she loved and trusted. They had done everything for her when her child came into the world, showering it with gifts and promises.

The two sat down. Robin sat down, with the baby in her hand. She was relieved for once that it wasn't Larisa.

"Where's you sister?" Cecilia asked.

"God knows," Robin said, never concerned for her wild sister.

Vegas went to the chase. "Doesn't matter. Anyway, there's a lot of heat out there. Giorgio's treading on dangerous waters. But don't fret. I'm going to set you guys up."

"Giorgio's staying with Dmitri, try to get enough money to help us out," Robin said.

"I'm going to get Giorgio out of there," Vegas said. "Trust me! Dmitri is a dangerous character and getting more dangerous by the hour."

"Well, if he's that dangerous, how are you going to get him out of this?"

"Let me worry about that. Just being the good mother that you are and take care of that boy."

Cecilia went to Vegas' shoulder. "And whatever you need, we're going to get it for you. All you need to do is ask."

"Thank you guys," Robin said happily. "I don't know what I'll do without you."

"Probably roll over and die," Vegas said as he laughed. Cecilia and Robin laughed with him.

* * *

Coming out of a church in the Tri-Cities were two groups of Dmitri's gang, including Cosine, Giorgio, and Slash. They were sent to find babies. So far they had taken almost a thousand babies, but had not found the one they were looking for. Cosine, who had been great on these missions, had risen up in ranks, being the youngest and quickest to ever move up high in the Underground Devils. They got into their vehicles. Then, leaving their trademark, the church was engulfed in flames.

Just a few more missions, Cosine thought, *and he was well on his way.*

As they drove fast from the church, they threw more bottles that caught fire to anything it came in contact with. Then, agent cars started coming out, chasing them through the street. The devils loved cruising fast and reckless, including Cosine, who was seeing a faster world with the buildup of speed. The chase went on for a while until one of the vehicles crashed into a long lamppost. All of Dmitri's gang came out with guns blazing at the agents. It was one big shootout, in which innocent ones ran for cover. The gang separated and the agents ran after them.

Cosine, separated from his crew, managed to head for a lake, away from the agents. He tried to catch his breath. He had been in this situation before, so nothing faded him.

Then, he heard a noise from the water. He turned around and shot the water. Now, he turned cold. Fear and adrenaline was rushing to his head. But all around him, there was silence. Nothing but the ripples in the water let him know something was there.

"Ah, nice hiding place!" A mysterious voice said.

Cosine turned around. He saw nothing, but someone punched him into the water. He got up and took out a knife from among his clothes. He swung it around. Something grabbed his arm and threw him down again. He moved his legs, but the figure took his leg and threw him right side up. He realized that he was fighting something invisible, but couldn't see him or her.

Then, the invisible fighter punched and kicked Cosine a few more times. Then, a super move flipped Cosine over to the deep. A few seconds later, an unconscious Cosine was raised into the air by the ghost fighter. The stranger appeared in true form.

"Cosine Secant! Tonight, your life changes forever," he said before gliding into the air, taking Cosine's lifeless body with him.

* * *

Vegas and Cecilia went out dancing at the X-Club. Since her breakup with Thorn, Cecilia has seen Vegas as a great stress reliever. A slow song came on and Vegas and Cecilia started moving slow. Both look into each other's eyes. Both were intensifying their situation with their closeness. Then, Cecilia relaxed on Vegas' shoulder. She really felt safe, like she could be herself and didn't have to question anyone about it.

Then, Vegas was able to get a female singer to sing a song for her, which sounded so sweet in Cecilia's ear. There was no other sound like it. Vegas smiled at Cecilia's face. Thorn could tell what he saw in her. She was really striking. It didn't matter about her past as a she-devil or the mean things that were done to her. Inside and out, Cecilia Broughton was the most beautiful woman in the world to Vegas.

After the X-Club, Vegas walked with Cecilia to her house. When they reached the door, they looked at each other, this time, more animated than on the dance floor.

"I must admit," Cecilia said. "I had a good time."

Vegas reacted. "See! I told you. There's hope, yet."

"Well, let me call it a night."

Cecilia kissed Vegas on the cheek.

"Good night," she said.

Cecilia walked inside her house as Vegas stared, making sure she made every step count. He looked at the night for a few seconds. The rain started to fall. He quickly went to the door, knocking. Cecilia opened it.

"I was wandering," Vegas said, "if I could come in for a while. For a drink or something."

Cecilia invited him inside. She fixed drinks in her kitchen as Vegas was checking out the home. She kept it clean and rich, he thought. Art was everywhere in the main room, mostly of seductive statues. Cecilia came back with some glasses and the wine bottle that it came with it.

"Nice home," Vegas said.

"Thanks," Cecilia said. "Normally I wouldn't be dealing with something like this. I don't like to spend so much, especially on a house. I would have been happier with something smaller. What about you? Where do you live?"

"The streets are my home."

"I can't see that. Someone as classy as you living on the street."

Vegas chucked. The alcohol was exciting him. "Why? Because I'm an angel and I have everything that's coming to me? That I'm supposed to present a certain image? Well, trust me. Sometimes it isn't always what it's cracked up to be."

"You hate what you do?" Cecilia asked. "You shouldn't. Your master is the Lord of the Universe. Mine, I don't know what the hell's going on with him."

"That's not a part of your life anymore."

"I know. Or maybe I don't know. Sometimes, I wonder if I'm doing the right thing. Sometimes, I wonder if it's even enough. I guess I just want someone to love me and not see me as some tramp from the street."

Vegas smirked. "That's bull!"

"What?"

"That's bull!" Vegas repeated. "Everything you just said was bull."

"What do you mean?"

"Why should you seek the love of someone else? Be true to yourself. Forget what everyone else said about you."

"This coming from angel boy?"

"That's right. This is coming from angel boy. I live how I live. Some of my comrades may not like it, but do you think I care? Frankly, you devils have it made better than we have it. We have to always fit some kind of quota. We have to act a certain way, dress a certain way, be a certain way. Sometimes, it's depressing. I can't see how Thorn's does it. Maybe it's one of those things that I'll never know."

Vegas took a look at Cecilia's body. She had luscious legs, Vegas thought. He was so entranced by it that he had to take out a cigarette and smoke it deeply. Cecilia was taking in some more alcohol before she saw Vegas staring.

"What is it?" Cecilia asked.

"Maybe you could clear something for me," Vegas said. "I've heard a rumor. I've heard that you used to be an exotic dancer. Is that true?"

"What if it is?"

"Well, is it?"

There was silence in Cecilia's side of the room. Vegas smiled.

"It is true?" he asked.

Cecilia was blushing a little. "Why you ask?" she asked.

"Because I was wondering if you could do a favor for me."

Cecilia took a drink of wine. "What?"

"Dance for me," Vegas said clearly.

"What?" Cecilia said shockingly.

"You've heard me. Dance for me."

"Here?"

"Well, I can't figure any other place to do it. We're in the privacy of your home. Why not?"

Cecilia had many things swimming in her head about this. But then, she smiled at Vegas. It was a deal. She got up, putting the glass away. She already had on her skirt. The legs were stretched out and Vegas was already aroused, but he would never tell her. Then, Cecilia went to another side of the house. With that came soothing and seductive music. Vegas smoked his cigarette coolly. Cecilia went to the wall, facing him. The first place she went for was her legs, then her midsection. She went under her shirt, unfastening it and exposing her breasts from her lingerie. Vegas smirked. Then, she went for the dress, which showed the curves of her body.

Then came the dance.

She had great moves, Vegas thought. At first, the dance was for Cecilia. She was feeling sexy and dangerous at the same time. The music inside her head was pulling her in and nothing else. She didn't know what she was doing, as if she wasn't herself anymore. She took a candid gander at Vegas, who had finished his cigarette. She went on top of him, started taking off his shirt, and caressed his chest. He loved it. He saw her eyes. They weren't the same. They were showing a sort of red glow. Vegas saw it happening. The devil in her was coming out, just what he wanted.

Then came the kiss. It was beautiful to the both of them and they both needed it. Within a few minutes, Vegas carried Cecilia in his arms and they were in Cecilia's bed, making love and taking their aggressions and frustrations out on their hormones. If Cecilia needed to take out some aggression, Vegas Armano told himself that he was more than happy to accommodate.

* * *

Thorn was working out with a determination near a forest. He was punching a long tree as hard as he could. The tree shook with every punch, each second looking as if it would fall. Even with the raining falling, it didn't stop the punches and the tension of his muscle.

Thorn Hawkins was on a mission, an internal mission to get his mind right as well as his body because he had a fight on his hands. The blow from his brother thanks to the influence of Dmitri fueled his anger. This would not be the same Thorn anyone knew when it was over.

And Dmitri Sheppard was a dead man.

* * *

Shadow was working with some weapons from outside. Gloria was doing experiments as Dorian was reading a sacred book. They knew there was something else to the mystery of Shadow's attacker or the attacks on the cities. The two look intently at the words. One that stuck out in their heads was "angel of destruction."

Was it evil to come? Dorian was fearful for what was about to happen, and it was the fact that he didn't know exactly what it was scared that him more.

* * *

As the rains fell, Erick Gold, Kim Silver, and Platinum were traveling, jumping on roofs like thieves in the night. Even the rain would not stop their activities. Death didn't take off-days in their eyes.

Looking from a roof was a spy, on one knee like a statue. It was time to follow them to see what was going on. In traveling on the roofs, following their paths, he could her the jokers laughing as loud as they could.

* * *

A knock was on the door. Robin opened it and saw Giorgio, with some bruises on his face. He came in slowly. Robin felt his face, but Giorgio grabbed her hand.

"What happened?" Robin asked.

"I don't want to talk about it," Giorgio said. "I… I just want to be with you tonight. I just want to hold you. I just want to be with you. Nothing else matters to me anymore."

Robin was worried. Giorgio could see it in her eyes, more at that moment than anything beforehand.

"It's getting dangerous out there," Robin said. "There's no telling what…"

"Nothing is going to happen to me."

Robin showed a little smile. It surprised her that he was being so brave when they have so much to lose.

"What if I told you that you may not be in Dmitri's gang any longer?" Robin asked.

Giorgio gave a smirk. "I don't know if it's possible, unless this someone's going to killed Dmitri."

"Don't worry. We can deal with Dmitri later. For now, you're here. My love, you're here. There's someone that wants to see you."

Robin got up and went into another room. When she came back, she brought the baby with her. She gave it to Giorgio. He held it and gently kissed it on the forehead with his soft lips. Robin sat by him and Giorgio put his arm around her close. Both heard the rain falling, which sounded so good in both of their ears.

ALLIANCE

Vegas woke up that morning in Cecilia's bed, but didn't get up. He took some time looking at the room and then at Cecilia still sleeping, hoping that it wasn't a dream and their wild night of passion really occurred. In seeing her pretty face, Vegas remembered meeting Cecilia for the first time.

Around the time, Thorn was starting his gladiator career for the Sodom Fires and Cecilia was starting her first term as captain of the cheerleaders. Vegas remembered kissing her hand and inside, was so jealous of Thorn for bagging a girl like her. Feeling only second best, he never felt that he would ever find another girl like Cecilia.

Truth was, there wasn't any woman like her. Cecilia Broughton was a woman unlike any other, a slick beauty who had faced dangerous times that added toughness to her demeanor. When Cecilia kissed him, Vegas was amazed, but guilty at the same time because he knew that Thorn still had a attraction for her. He knew that when he came back from wherever he was at this point, he would have to tell him. For now, he would vast in the glow of romancing Cecilia.

When Cecilia got up and went on top of Vegas, kissing him all over his chest, he was reassured.

"I must say," Cecilia said sensually. "I really needed that last night."

"I'm happy to oblige, sweetheart," Vegas said.

"Although I wasn't expecting it."

"Neither was I."

Vegas smiled. He was happy to know that Cecilia didn't get angry or pushed him out of bed. Something inside of her was pleased that Vegas' warm body was beside hers. But then, a thought came to Vegas' mind, something serious. He took his shirt from among the covers and put it on.

"I have some things to take care of for Robin," Vegas said. "If I get done in time, we can do another nighter."

"I would like that."

Cecilia and Vegas kissed, preparing for another session of passion.

Vegas was going to be busy today. So many demands. But one thing about Vegas was that he was used to a lot of demands as well as making sure they were carried out. Even though Vegas was considered a rebel, he did have a good heart, but only a few considerate people like Robin or Thorn could ever bring it out of him, especially when the person he was going to ask for help was the last person he ever wanted to see: Dmitri Sheppard.

As a young boy, Vegas grew up among priests. His father, a fellow priest himself, was strict on him when it came to the one true God. He would always tell him about the Holy Books. He was the only one who told him about his destiny that he was to become an angel of God. For a time, until he reached his teens, Vegas followed the comments of his father, always telling him that God loved him and he would end up doing a great service for him. But as soon as he reached his teens and began to separate himself from the world of the priests, he became a part of the streets, where devils ran rampant. It was unusual for an angel to make friends, or even business partners with devils.

One of those people happened to be Dmitri Sheppard.

The first time Vegas met him, Dmitri Sheppard was already hitting the road to master criminal. His skills in the black arts were improving with each passing day. He managed to do every mischievous thing from breaking windows to starting fires to drive-by shootings and rebel fighting. The teenage Dmitri was into everything, and Vegas respected him. Around the time he was becoming friends with Dmitri, he had met Thorn Hawkins, but it wasn't until he reached college when Thorn would become closer to a pure friend than Dmitri.

When Vegas and Dmitri met and became friends, Vegas got involved in the craziness of the devils. Sometimes, he would make deals for him that carried on to their adult lives. His greatest racket was the street drugs. Vegas never loved sin, but at the same time, he didn't like the holiness and the aura the priests believed. But like his father had told him, his destiny had already been painted for him. He was to become an angel even if it killed him. Vegas had no choice, so in defiance, he got closer to Dmitri.

The two men never liked each other simply because of their different affiliations. So most wonder what it was in their relationship that made them connect. The answer was that both were addicted to two things: freedom to have a will to do anything, and making a profit.

When Vegas met Thorn, he was already knee deep with Dmitri. Then, Thorn introduced Vegas to his friends, who were innocent and benevolent. This opened something in Vegas only his father could do. With that, he disassociated himself with Dmitri, leaving it strictly business and nothing more. He devoted his power for good.

But on this day, that was not to be. For the sake of his friend Robin Jenkins, her lover, and her child, Vegas had to forget about the past, forget about Dmitri's manipulative charm, forget about the respect he had shown him and vice versa every since he was an teenager, and become the devil he pretended to be for a long time.

Vegas went into Dmitri's office. Dmitri, working on some papers and his top-secret project, went to Vegas and hugged him.

"Vegas, partner," Dmitri said. "What brings you here? I mean after our last encounter, I didn't think you would come back to see me."

"I was just busy," Vegas said. "I came here for a favor."

"Why am I'm not surprised? What is it?"

"I need some money. More than usual."

"And how much is more than usual?"

"About a few hundred thousand."

Dmitri knew that Vegas took risks, but at that question, he was thinking if he knew what he was doing.

"Are you crazy?" he asked.

"You know I'm good for it," Vegas said. "Besides, I'm making more deals for your gang."

Dmitri shook his head. "Vegas, Vegas, Vegas! What am I going to do with you?"

"I don't know," Vegas said ironically.

Dmitri stayed silent for a few seconds. "I'll think about it."

"Well, take your time."

Vegas got up and was about to leave.

"Hey, I was wondering." Vegas pointed to the door. "On my way up here, I saw some babies being taken in to different rooms. You mind telling me what that's all about?"

"Oh, that! Just experimenting."

"On what?"

"Nothing. No big deal. We'll talk later."

"I guess."

Vegas left the office. Then, Slash and Essence entered. They looked at Dmitri strangely as Dmitri lounged back in his chair.

"What did he want?" Slash asked, already being fueled up for damage, which didn't take much.

Dmitri rubbed his head. "What does Vegas always want?"

Essence said, "We have over thousand of babies here and none of them have it."

Dmitri shouted. "Where is that damn child?"

Dmitri threw something across the room that almost hit Essence.

"What's the big deal?" Essence asked. "I mean, it's just a child. And besides, don't you have to give it to whoever wants it anyway?"

"For what?" Dmitri enforced. "The child is mine when you find it."

"What brought this on?"

"What is it to you?" Dmitri said with an attitude. "Go back and find that child. And don't creep back up here until you do."

Slash left.

"Essence?"

Essence stopped. Dmitri took her arm gently and put her close to his cheek. He gave her a kiss that barely touched her. "Do me a favor. Watch Vegas for me. Watch him carefully. I don't trust that little sneak.

Essence left out the office, not fully condoning what Dmitri was doing and why he was now obsessed with getting this child.

Giorgio was walking up the hallway to Dmitri's office. Slash was walking the opposite direction when they met.

"Giorgio, there you are," Slash said. "I need you tonight. Cosine's been missing for quite some time. We have to find him."

Giorgio didn't know what was worse, getting deeper into the gang or going to find a crazy Cosine so he could go through the nightmares all over again.

"I'm there," Giorgio said.

Slash noticed that Giorgio was a little shaky. "You okay?"

"Fine," Giorgio said, tensing his muscles. "Why?"

"Just look different, that's all."

Slash left. Larisa walked to Giorgio. He hoped this wasn't going to be another field day, but before he could go another way and escaped her, Larisa took his arm roughly and took him to a secret room, not drawing any attention to herself.

This was the last straw for Giorgio. Larisa was taking this to the extreme. As for Larisa, she was tired of chasing him, tired of playing hard to get or playing the game of romance. She was resorting to conquer by force.

Larisa threw Giorgio into the room and slammed the door.

"Hello, Giorgio," Larisa said, cracking her knuckles.

Giorgio saw that this wasn't the same Larisa from before. He could see her muscle tensed up.

"Hello," Giorgio said softly.

Giorgio tried to walk on, but Larisa grabbed his arm again. She ravaged him, sinking her nails into his chest.

"Look," Larisa said with a rage of sexuality growing in her, "you can't keep doing this. I won't let you. So you might as well quit trying to resist."

Giorgio seized his wrist. "Larisa, get this through your head. I don't want anything to do with you. Now, you may be one of Dmitri's main officers, but when it comes to personal things, you don't run that or me. Now, leave me alone."

Giorgio pushed her away, but with quick reflexes, Larisa grabbed the back of his shirt, rougher than the last time.

"That was a bad move, Giorgio," Larisa said, with her teeth turning into fangs. "No one says no to me. You'll learn, young buck. You'll learn."

Giorgio ran away. Essence came into the room. She stopped silent, wondering what was the war about. Larisa closed her mouth and rubbed her lips.

"You're okay?" Essence asked.

Larisa was silent, feeling the rush. Essence knew immediately who's to blame. She asked, "What am I? Did I just turn ugly or something?"

Essence touched Larisa's face and into her intense eyes.

"Please!" Essence said. "You're as beautiful as I remember. Don't ever say you're not. If you want, I can see what's going with Giorgio. It's my job, anyway. Don't fret. You'll have that man eating from your hand in no time. I guarantee it."

"If you do that, I'll be so grateful."

"I'll take you up on that offer."

Essence left. Larisa turned to a mirror that was near her and look at herself. She saw that she was changing. Her face had become red, the true essence of the devil. If Giorgio saw her like this, she knew for sure that Giorgio would never set eyes on her again. Larisa had never had a problem with her conquering beauty. And the woman who had bagged Giorgio, had better fear, Larisa thought.

* * *

Shadow found out from the time he stayed at the luxurious mansion that it belonged to Ankaro Lindbergh. It was his sort of command center in Greenwood. To others, he got it from being a rich businessman, but the Almighty Lord gave him that title. He was standing on the large terrace, looking at the great view of mountains and waterfalls in the distance, part of the reason he chose the strip of land, and talking with Dorian and Gloria.

"I think there's more to this than some reckless gang and murders," Gloria said.

"What we think is whatever's going on, Dmitri is definitely in this," Dorian said.

"I'm sure he is," Ankaro said, not paying close attention.

Gloria said, "There's something else. Something I didn't tell Dorian. I read something in a book that was interesting. It has nothing to do what we're dealing with, but I thought you might tell me something about it. It was talking about an angel of destruction. It read, 'behold, you give me a devil of creation and I will give you an angel of destruction.' "

"It was his last words," Ankaro whispered.

Gloria knew he was paying attention now. "Who?"

"Or was there really last words?"

"What's going on?" Dorian asked Gloria.

"I don't know," Gloria said.

Ankaro sensed something brewing within everything Gloria was talking about. More than either of them knew.

Could it be true? Was I anticipating this? The angel of destruction!

Ankaro thought about an image of someone who will lead the new human beings and cause chaos. He had nightmares about this. He saw fire burning all around him and angels and devils kneeling before him, this being who would be known as the angel of destruction.

Ankaro knew of this myth. He had heard the story. But he never thought it could happen. An evil everlasting was unheard of. But it would make sense. What better way for a being like that to rule so viciously than the child of an angel and a devil, a child who carried the genes of good and evil?

Ankaro stopped thinking with Dorian came to him.

"Everything okay?" Dorian asked.

"Everything's fine," Ankaro said. "I have to go back to my quarters. Take care."

Ankaro walked away quickly without word as Dorian and Gloria stared.

"Do you get that?" Dorian asked Gloria.

"No! He's hiding something," Gloria said. "Do you think he'll tell us?"

"Doesn't matter. We have bigger things to worry about."

* * *

Dmitri was reading more of the same book in his office. His phone rang and he picked it up. A sinister voice came on the phone.

"Who is this?"

We need to meet.

"It's you again."

Meet me at the demon wasteland. That way, we'll be away from all the attention.

Dmitri hanged up the phone hard. He knew who it was.

* * *

Essence and Larisa were in a vehicle together near several stores and a large restaurant with eager eyes, looking out for anything suspicious. Larisa needed to get her mind out of Giorgio, so Essence took her along on this mission. Larisa knew that she could always count on Essence to cheer her up. She understood her. In Essence's mind, she didn't have the beauty that Larisa had, but she did have the common sense Larisa lacked.

"What makes you think they'll be here?" Larisa said, finding lookout boring.

"Vegas makes some of his deals in this area," Essence said. "It's one of his special spots. If there's anywhere something would go down with him, he'll bring it here."

"I hope Giorgio's here also."

"If he's here, then we'll know. Trust."

Essence saw two people walking together to the large restaurant. It was Vegas and Cecilia.

"There he is," Essence said. "But look at this."

Essence pointed to the curvy Cecilia.

"Tell me that girl doesn't look familiar to you," she said.

Larisa looked at her closer. "Cecilia Broughton? I thought she was going out with Thorn Hawkins. What's she doing with Vegas? Well, I see she hasn't lost her touch. She still has the skills."

"I knew something's going down. I feel it."

Larisa saw another familiar face going in with Vegas and Cecilia. It was Giorgio.

"Giorgio?"

"This is straight crazy!" Essence commented.

"I'm about to go see."

Larisa was about to get out the car, but Essence stopped her.

"Wait!" Essence said. "Lord Dmitri said to do nothing but watch. I tell you one thing. He's not going to like this."

"We'll get a better look if we get closer."

As soon as Larisa was about to get out again, Essence's phone went off. She answered it.

"Essence? When? Now? We was about… Alright fine."

"What's going on?"

"We got to go."

Essence and Larisa drove off.

* * *

Vegas, Cecilia, Giorgio, and three others, who were leaders of the Dog, Cat, and Bird gangs, sat together and talk. The gangs were the most ruthless of the New World, who emerged from the burrows between the Old and the New World. The gangs were only looking out for themselves, coming to agreement that neither one of the gangs would raid on each other's territories.

54

"Surprising we meet here," the Dog leader said.

"Sorry we had to meet so secretly," Vegas apologized.

"Normal for us," the Cat leader agreed.

The Bird leader looked at Giorgio with an eagerness to kill him. "Who is he?"

Vegas went to the point before the leaders got edgy. "That's what we got to talked about. I'm sure you have heard of recent attacks made by Dmitri and his gang. Now it seems that he has a new agenda and your gangs might be in danger. Dmitri will do anything to make sure he gets what he wants. And he'll have no problem wiping you all out if he have to."

The Cat leader said, "He comes my way, I'll make sure it doesn't happen a second time."

The Dog leader agreed. "Same for me. I'll defend my honor with my life and I'm sure my men will do the same."

Cecilia touched Giorgio's hand. "This is Giorgio Martel. He's a part of Dmitri's gang. However, he has a child that needs to be protected. I'm sure some of your gang's children are being taken."

The Cat leader hissed. "Cold-blooded. He's nothing but cold-blooded. Taking babies. Why would he do that?"

"I feel that if we work together, we'll defeat them," Vegas said, breaking the ice.

"Them? They're others?" The Bird leader asked.

"We also feel that Dmitri has someone else working with him. Someone like a silent partner. So we need to get rid of them as well."

The Locust leader said, "Whatever we have to do."

"One more thing," Cecilia said. "Whatever we talked about here, stays here."

"Already forgotten," the Dog leader said.

To seal the alliance, Vegas paid for their food. All the while that Vegas was there, he was thinking that now he was in trouble. He had become a target.

WASTELAND

There were a number of wastelands stranded around Greenwood.

In this particular wasteland, miles away from the Tri-Cities, it was unique because the wasteland was once a grand city with skyscrapers and bridges. Swampy water, weeds, flytrap-like trees, and remains of shattered statues from acid rains remain.

Despite the damage, it was perfect ground for Thorn Hawkins.

Thorn was practicing his fighting skills in a sophisticated, landscaped wasteland, full of destroyed buildings and relics of the old world. For several weeks after his brother turned on him, he was in isolation, spending that time on fighting and meditating. His muscles were larger, his punches were stronger, his feet were faster, and his mind was clearer. He had to get his life back together at any cost. One thing he knew was that with his Lord following him, he knew that it wouldn't be long before he could get his brother back and reconciled with Cecilia. He missed her so much and regretted everyday that he broke it off with her. There was no telling what she was doing or going through without him. She had always relied on him.

Suddenly, he heard noises. Escaping his train of thought, he traveled around, staying out of sight. From a bush, he saw people coming his way. They were heading for a building in large numbers. Noises of shouts and talking were evident to Thorn. It was Dmitri and his Underground Devils gang. Thorn decided to stop doing what he was doing and followed them. Maybe at that instant, he could get his revenge. On his back, he had a gun, the signature gun he was going to use to kill Dmitri when he saw him.

Meanwhile, the Underground Devils traveled through the swampy place, acknowledging the once-grand architecture and complaining at their present condition. As the gang circled around, making sure the exotic flies that were around them didn't bite them, Dmitri was walking calmly and carefully.

"This is creepy," Essence said. "I don't like this."

"I think we'll being set up," Slash said. "Why did they want to meet us here? And what is all this stuff?"

Dmitri stood motionless. He covered his nose.

"This place is a tomb," he said. "A tribute of the Old World. Who would have believe?"

Suddenly, an arrow shot up in the air and landed near Dmitri's feet. Then, more arrows gliding through the air landed around the gang. One actually struck a devil's leg and even when he was screaming in pain, Dmitri stood his ground. Suddenly, men in dark cloaks surrounded them.

"Reapers," Dmitri whispered.

The three main Reapers: Erick, Kim, and Platinum, came out to meet them, standing on one of the chipped skyscrapers.

"Lord Dmitri," Erick screamed. "You made it. We were worried."

"I don't see why," Dmitri shouted, matching the range of his voice with Erick. "What is this all about? I have things to do."

"Like stealing on our little fortune."

"What are you talking about?" Dmitri said acting sweetly.

Kim uttered out, "The child! You're getting that obsession. I can see it in your eyes. You want the child for yourself."

"That's all?" Dmitri asked, not amused by them or what they know. They were right. He wanted the child. He needed the child. And he would even face the Reapers to do so, knowing he would have been making a mistake. No angel or devil could fight or possibly kill the Reapers.

Essence went to Dmitri's shoulder. "What is she talking about, Lord Dmitri?"

Kim jumped off of the skyscraper.

"Oh! They don't know?" Kim said. "Who are you going to kill first once you find the child, Lord Dmitri? Is it Essence here? Or is it Slash?"

"Shut up," Slash said.

Kim clapped in humor as the Reapers stood still.

Slash took out a massive sword from his back. The rest of his gang did the same with their weapons, ready to die. The other Reapers did the same with their swords.

Hiding in a safe place, Thorn got ready to fire his gun at Dmitri. He didn't see the Reapers except for Kim. He was shocked when he saw her. What was the Reapers' purpose in this fight, he thought. But there was no time to think. Nothing was going to stop him. He had Dmitri right where he wants him. But then, he noticed something. He noticed that for some reason, Dmitri might be involved in a trap.

"You want a war with me?" Dmitri shouted at the Reapers. "I'll give you one. You mess with the wrong devil."

A fellow soldier came to Dmitri. "We have a problem Lord Dmitri from the distance."

"What are you talking about?"

Suddenly, there were a few explosions near the area, killing some of the Underground Devil soldiers from both sides.

Dmitri circled around. "What the hell?"

More explosions happened. Then came the sound of running and shouting. Dmitri saw it and couldn't believe it. The demon, locust, and dragon gangs ran from all sides to them, killing them off. A battle has begun. Erick and Kim escaped from the fighting. Dmitri went after them.

He ran to another part of the wasteland. He stopped all of a sudden when he saw a familiar face. It was Shadow Fades, holding his gun.

"Where do you think you're going?" Shadow said.

Dmitri was shocked. "Shadow? Can't be!"

"Looks like that assassin you sent didn't finish me off."

"They didn't kill you? I should have known. So, what are you going to do, kill me? For what? You have no reason."

Thorn entered, pointing the gun at Dmitri from the other side.

"But I do," Thorn said.

"Great," Dmitri said. "Here you are."

"Where's my brother, Dmitri?"

"As much as I want to say nothing, I don't know where he is. But if I did know, trust me, he will die just like you will for trying this."

Dmitri looked at Shadow, and then at Thorn. He thought to himself for a second. "Well," Dmitri said, "I guess there's one thing I can do?"

Suddenly, Dmitri used one of his powers and made a reflection of himself. Shadow and Thorn thought he was attacking and shot at him. Shadow was shot in the shoulder while Thorn got a scar on the face. Thorn went to him, covering his scar. Laughter was heard from Dmitri, who escaped into the shadows.

* * *

In another part of the wasteland, Erick and Kim were alone. Then, they saw two people looking at them. It was Dorian and Gloria, with wings sprouted out.

"Reapers!" Dorian shouted.

Erick stared at them. "The angels. What are they doing here?"

Gloria said, "It's starting to make sense. It was them."

"I don't like this," Dorian said.

Erick and Kim struck and a fight began between the Reapers and the Greenwood Angels was underway. At first, there was an even fight, but the Reapers proved to be stronger, crippling the angels' defenses no matter what it was.

"Let's put the final blow to them," Erick said.

"Right, darling," Kim agreed.

Erick and Kim put their hands together. A glow of light grew from them. The light was so strong, Dorian and Gloria couldn't see them anymore. They covered their eyes, a big mistake. A beam shot out and an explosion along with smoke appeared. Erick and Kim smiled, but the smiles turn to frowns when they saw someone. Someone had blocked the blast.

It was Victor Marcus, *in his Reaper attire.*

"The Black Reaper," Erick said, backing away in small steps.

"You guys don't stop," Victor said in his disturbing but confident voice. "Now face the master."

From his hand, a sword appeared. He swayed and twisted it without flinching. Victor took the fight to Kim and Erick. Dorian and Gloria started watching, amazed at the quickness of all three Reapers. But in watching carefully, it was Victor who had the upper hand, holding his own against them. The way he was moving his sword compared to theirs, something told the angels not only did Victor knew them, but they were close once. When prove too quick and powerful, Erick and Kim escaped into the sky. Victor stood there, with the sword disappearing from his hand.

Gloria went to him. "That was impressive."

Victor turned around and swung the sword at her, pointing it very close to her neck. Gloria got a little worried as she was staring into Victor's fiery eyes.

"It's not finished," Victor said. "They have to be stopped. You have to stop them."

Dorian said, "We know that, but what about you? How do we know we have to stop you, too?"

"You just might."

Victor jumped into the air and disappeared, leaving in smoke. Gloria and Dorian watched as the alliance cheered in victory. Shadow and Thorn went to them. The alliance had their victory for now. The concern for Victor Marcus would have to come later.

* * *

Dmitri, in a vengeful mood, started throwing objects around near his gang, who watched and moved whenever the objects came near them. This was the angriest Dmitri had ever been in a long time. He almost forgot for a time what it felt like. He knew it was the child motivating the anger. He hoped that when he find the child, it would be worth it because between the Reapers, Thorn, and Shadow, a crying child sounded great to him.

"What the hell happened out there?" Dmitri shouted furiously.

Everyone was silent.

"Anyone?"

Dmitri took a breath to calm himself, thinking he was better than this. He was better than the fury he was feeling.

He continued. "How did the demons, the dragons, and the locusts know about this?"

Silence.

"Still, no one knows? Alright, so if this is what they want, then fine. Slash gathered an army together. Tell them that we're going to run through every town and torch everything and kill everyone until that child is found, until the parents are found, and most of all, until their little negotiator is found. Since we're nothing but jokes to everyone, time for them to see who they're really messing with. The King of the Devils may have lost the first war, but we will not lose a second one. Hell will have its fury again. And Lord Dmitri Sheppard will bring it."

* * *

The Tri-Cities was becoming a war zone. This time, it was Dmitri flicking the switch. Their actions ranged from burnings to shootings in which lives were taken. The Underground Devils had become more dangerous as ever humanly possible. Nothing in this world was ready to face them. So far, the Dragons and the Locusts suffered the worst causalities. The Demons were still in the fight.

Meanwhile, Giorgio and Robin were in bed together with their sleeping baby, not trying to worry about the events going on outside. Both were as close to each other and their child as they could possibly be. They heard noise from outside. It was the actions between gangs. Robin was more afraid for Giorgio than even before. She was thinking why Vegas didn't come through with her promise.

Giorgio said, "Now Dmitri's at war with everyone."

"We have to get out of here," Robin said.

"And where will we go? We have no more hiding places."

Suddenly, a hard knock was on the door. Giorgio quickly got up, with a gun in his hand, and looked out the door. He put his gun up and opened the door. It was Cecilia, who rushed in and hugged him. Robin walked in, with the child that she woke up.

"My God!" Cecilia said, relieved. "I'm so glad you're okay. And you too, Robin? I thought something might happen to him after…"

"We're fine," Robin said.

"Vegas told me to tell you to get out of here."

"And where will we go?" Giorgio asked, with his arm around Robin.

"I've found you a place," Cecilia said. "We don't know if it's good or not, so until then, you can stay here, under watch. After that, Giorgio, you stay away from Dmitri. Both of you!"

"I can't," Giorgio said. "He'll know and I won't put Robin or my child in danger. I sacrificed myself for them if I have to."

"It's nice you want to be brave," Cecilia said, "but this thing with your boss is getting out of hand."

Robin asked, "Where's Vegas now?"

"I haven't seen him since our meeting with the gang leaders." Her thoughts went to the alliance. "I feel sorry that they have to suffer through all this."

What was worse was Vegas was alone in the mist of it!

SACRIFICE OF A SOLDIER

DMITRI WAS DRINKING WINE, WALKING AROUND, AND FEELING CONFIDENT ABOUT the actions his gang had made. He loved the thrill of fire and blood flowing from the bodies of his enemies. He loved that he decided who lives and dies. It was a statement to the Reapers. Inside, though, he knew that in fight Erick and Kim, he would be fighting a legion of them, and he wasn't trained to fight a power like that.

Essence entered in to see him, ruining his private happiness. Dmitri just shook it off and return to his serious mode.

"What is going on?" Dmitri asked calmly. "I want to have my privacy."

Essence was getting worried. "I should have come with this sooner."

"With what?"

Essence took her time to answer. She knew that lately, her boss, almost her father figure, was troubled about losing to the Reapers and the combined gangs, even though he had the upper hand at the moment.

"I know who told the gangs about us and who stole some of your finances," she said. "Larisa and I found out. It was Vegas Armano."

"Vegas?"

Dmitri stared into Essence's eyes, bringing fear in her.

"Vegas!" He screamed.

Dmitri threw the glass he was drinking out of at her, but slightly missed. Some of the shattered glass fell on Essence's hair.

"It was Vegas the whole time," he said. "And you said nothing?"

"We wanted to be sure," Essence said. "We have word that Vegas is hiding out near the wasteland with the Wasteland Dogs."

Slash entered while they talk.

"Slash!" Dmitri said, turning the attention around. "Good you're here. Gather the men. We're going back to the wasteland."

"There's something else," Essence said. "Our old friend, Cecilia Broughton was in on this as well. Her and Vegas were working together."

"Well, we'll get rid of Vegas. And I'll let you think of a good punishment for our old friend, Cecilia."

* * *

Cecilia walked along a lonely street, thinking of her situation in helping Robin and Giorgio. If she didn't fell alone then, she was feeling it now. Thorn was not there to comfort and give her encouraging words. Now, Vegas was out of sight and in grave danger. Plus, she wasn't known as a physical fighter.

Suddenly, turning around, she spotted a car stop in front of her, watching over her every shoulder. Some of Dmitri's gang, wearing their black and red covered in black masks, popped out of the large car and kidnapped Cecilia, even though she fought hard to get away. They got her in the car and drove as fast as they could. The masked devils were able to knock her unconscious. One of them took off their mask. It was Larisa.

When Cecilia woke up slightly from her injury, she found out she was chained up, with legs and arms spread out in a room that looked like an old strip club she used to work at before changing her life. She was feeling queasy, worse than she did when she was kidnapped. She woke up to see someone looking at her. Larisa entered with a smirk on his face. In the clear version that she could get from her eyes, Larisa was not a little girl she knew then. She had become a woman with a lethal body.

"I was hoping you would wake up," Larisa said.

"Where… where am I?" Cecilia asked in her weariness.

Larisa raised her arms to the surroundings and turned around to make sure Cecilia saw it carefully.

"Don't tell me this place doesn't look familiar to you," Larisa said. "This was your home for a long time until you decided to change, forgetting the people who helped you when you were in need. Funny how some of us forget so quickly when something, or someone good comes in."

Larisa walked to her and caressed her face. "You used to be beautiful, baby. Now look at you. A disgrace! What a shame! Too bad you will suffer like Vegas will when Dmitri finds him."

"I hope…" Cecilia cleared her throat. She whispered, "I hope… I hope Vegas kills your boss, and… then comes after you."

Larisa smiled. "How cute!"

She kissed Cecilia in the lips, but Cecilia resisted and spitted in her face. Larisa slowly wiped it off, but quickly slapped Cecilia in the face with the back of her hand. Larisa was grinning while holding her hand. Something in her wanted to do that for a long time, but Cecilia was not faded. Her face had no excitement.

Larisa grabbed her face and said sensually, "You know, before I kill you, I'm going to let the boys have some fun with you. I'm sure when they do, it bring back some memories, little whore."

Larisa walked pass her and left. Then, three other young devils entered the room. One of them released her from the chain, but they carried her to another secret room and to a sort-of stage, where one by one, they laid her on it. Cecilia looked up and her unclear vision saw glasses and candles being lit. She may not have seen it visibly, but she knew what this room was. She saw it in her past and later on in her nightmare.

With that, one by one, they came on top of her and raped her. Cecilia didn't fight back, taking the abuse, feeling inside that this was who she was all along. She was hoping to find out later that this was all a dream and she would wake up with her life back to normal. As one after another reach their peaks, they started cheering. At that point, the only person she was thinking about was Vegas and what was happening to him?

After the rape, the devils took Cecilia back into the car and near some open ground, brought her out and put her body there before driving off. She struggled hard to get up. She was looking at her scars and instead of crying, she just stroked them.

Cecilia was walking the street again. For some reason, the pain soothed her. She had seen worse in her past.

She remembered using the powers of seduction to get what she wanted. At that time, she had everything. She was popular, although ridiculed at the same time. She and her band mate, Larisa Rhodes, knew how to play the game with the best of them, and they played for keeps. Larisa gave her the kiss of life and death, the power she carried for anyone anxious to change their life. It was this kiss and every kiss from that point on that embedded her forever to them.

The difference was that Cecilia was doing this so she could get her life together. She had plans bigger than Larisa's dream world. Larisa, however, was playing the game full-time, which only worsened when she met the handsome and charismatic Dmitri Sheppard.

In that, Cecilia joined Dmitri's gang to watch out for her friend. Being in the life of the carnal wild wasn't fun anymore. She turned to a life of petty crime. Larisa ended up in a worse road, getting addicted on different drugs. Bit by bit, Cecilia was losing her friend. In the end, Larisa was too deep to escape, so Cecilia had no choice but to escape from the gang, leaving her friend to the wolves.

Nothing but contempt reigned Larisa Rhodes' world. Perhaps it was the wrong move, but when Cecilia met Thorn, Vegas, and Robin, it erased the doubt. Larisa would have to do her best, Cecilia thought, to escape Dmitri's wrath. But the power of evil is stronger than anyone would believe.

Looking at her wound on her side she had when she was younger, it stood as a reminder of reassurance that her friend could not escape, and for now on, accepted the fate. Cecilia realized that there was no way would she accept hers,. She must find Vegas or Thorn or someone. Her remaining friends were the only ones that matter now. She must live for them.

* * *

Vegas was talking with the Wasteland Dog leader he knew from the alliance as an army surrounded them, guarding their territory. He had formed a close relationship with the demons, but was afraid that they were getting too close to him, now that he was a target for Dmitri. Vegas could see demons on top of trees, in the distance, and lurking in hiding places he never would have considered.

"I can't believe it," the Demon leader said. "We really pissed him off."

"I know," Vegas said. "I'm really put you in a bad spot."

"We've been in worse spots before. We're going to fight 'till we die. And we're going to do what we said we're going to do. Protect your friends. What are you going to do?"

"I don't know. Whatever I do, I have to do it quick."

Suddenly, explosions were heard. Vegas was startled. Then, shots rang near them.

"What was that?" Vegas asked.

"They're here."

More explosions occurred.

"Hide!"

Vegas and the demon leader ran out and saw demon soldiers fighting against the devils of Dmitri's gang, with Lord Dmitri leading them with a vengeance. There were at least a hundred more than when they were fighting the alliance, going up against three hundred Wasteland Dogs. The demon leader ran on while Vegas hid out of sight. Weapons were used, fists were flying, and bodies fell. Dmitri pushed on until afterwards, the only demon among them left was the leader. Dmitri went to him with a blade in his hand.

"Where's Vegas, if you value your life," Dmitri said as he was swinging his sword.

"I don't think so!"

The leader spit in his face and like a reflex, Dmitri cut his head off. He walked on, observing the trees and debris on the ground.

"Where are you Vegas?" Dmitri roared. "I know you're here. There's no one here to help you, so why don't you just show yourself? I swear to you I won't do anything. I'll just ask you why you betrayed me? That's all."

Slash went to Dmitri and whispered to him, then pointed him to a spot. Dmitri took Slash's large gun he was carrying and pointed it at a huge tree. He started shooting at it and Vegas ran out, showing himself to the gang with a long, wooden cross in his hands. Dmitri stopped shooting.

"There you are," Dmitri said. "You're in trouble now."

Vegas caught his breath, but then slowly started laughing.

"And what is so funny?" Dmitri asked.

Vegas stopped laughing. "You… You're funny, Dmitri."

Dmitri entertained him. "How, Vegas?"

With more snickering, Vegas said, "You will not get that child. I'll protect it with my life."

Dmitri was not shocked that Vegas knew about the child. He brushed his shoulders. "I don't see why. What do you have to gain from this? But I have to give it to you. That thing you did? Bringing the gangs together to go up against me? That was brilliant. I mean really! Couldn't think of it myself. But what has it done for you? They're all dead. You have no one. Not even your Savior will save you. He doesn't care about you. No one does. He's left you all on your own. You could have been better off with us."

Vegas closed his eyes and whispered to himself, "Lord, I know I'm not the greatest angel in the world, but let me use you one more time. Use me to fight this devil. Let me die fighting for you."

Vegas held the cross to the sky. His angel wings sprouted as his power grew.

He shouted, "Let me do this for you, Father! Let me destroy this evil once and for all."

Dmitri and his gang laughed.

"Cut the bullshit," he said. "Give me the child!"

"Never," Vegas yelled.

"Okay! Since you put it that way. Kill him."

The gang stood together and started firing their guns upon him, neither one stopping until they were out of bullets. When it was all said and done, Vegas was still standing, but staggering, with scars on him. Vegas dropped the cross and brought out a sword from his hand and pointed it at Dmitri. He started breathing hard. He knew that using that power to dodge the gunfire took a lot out of him.

Dmitri was amazed. "Still standing, huh? Everyone step back. He's mine."

The gang got back until Dmitri was standing alone. Vegas charged after him. Dmitri took his hands back. When the impact came, a large energy blast formed that pushed everyone back. Vegas and Dmitri got up and faced each other again.

The fight went on for seconds with each one giving equal blows. Vegas wounded him in the arm and Dmitri fell to the ground. From that, the rest of the army charged after him and Vegas fought them, being able to beat them. In his mind, Vegas felt that he had a chance. He would live another day. He would see Cecilia and Thorn and Robin again.

It wasn't until Essence came from behind and stabbed Vegas in the back with her knife. Vegas turned to see the knife on his side and the blood from the blade. Vegas pushed Essence away. Other soldiers came forward and even with the wound, Vegas was still as valiant as before. He would not give up until death caught up with him.

From that, the rest of the army attacked. The numbers were too much. Vegas knew no matter how well he slashed, he had no choice but to submit to the wrath of Dmitri. One of the soldiers got Dmitri up and he walked over to the army as they continued their struggle. The only person not fighting was Giorgio Martel, who could only watch his savior died before his eyes. Larisa noticed it as well, but paid it no attention as she was laughing from the bloodlust inside of her.

* * *

Thorn was sleeping and woke up as he heard screams in his mind.

"Oh, no! Vegas."

Thorn got up and ran out. Something in his mind told him that he needed to go to the wasteland. When he got there, Thorn walked around and saw the carnage left over. Bodies of several devils, but almost all the Wasteland Dogs lay before him. He touched a few of their bodies.

Suddenly, he saw a sight that changed his mood and made him sick. It was the body of Vegas Armano, nailed to a cross. He walked slowly to it. A message was nailed near his feet. It said "DIE ALL WHO CROSS LORD DMITRI." Thorn put his head on the cross and tapped it with his head in sadness before he fell on his knees.

"It was inevitable. What happened to Vegas!" Victor Marcus, in a black suit, stood on an unmarked gravesite and stared at Vegas, showing no emotion.

Thorn turned to see Victor's face. "You knew what happened?"

Victor jumped off from the gravesite. "My guess was Dmitri." He nodded his head. "Nasty. Creative but nasty."

"You could have at least help the man out, not make fun of him," Thorn said as he raised himself up.

"What makes you think I wouldn't have killed him? Or you for that matter?"

Thorn started getting cautious of this Victor Marcus. He never forgot the henchman that attacked him at Sodom's locker room. This was the first time that he talked to him face to face. He wanted to know what fear Vegas found in him.

Victor continued. "What Vegas did was his decision and his alone. No one would have stopped him once it was all accounted for. And as for the amusement of this, as you so put it? Let me tell you something about that. I have seen more death than anyone can record their memories of life. Some were taken from my own hands. I had to feel the pain of people as they blamed me for their lives going nowhere. Sooner or later, bit-by-bit, death becomes… this amusing thing to you. Yeah! It becomes one big joke. And you feel you have to keep doing it for the joke to continue to be funny to you."

"Didn't know you had it so rough," Thorn said sarcastically.

"Well, it doesn't matter now," Victor said and he pointed to Vegas' lifeless body. "This, on the other hand, presents a problem for me. Not only do I have to deal with my comrades, but now I have to deal with that devil and his gang. I could use the help, Thorn."

"Now you want my help, after your henchman attacked me?"

"You want to save the rest of your friends, don't you? Well, I feel you'll need me. No! I know you'll need me. Along with Dorian, Gloria, and Shadow."

"You know about them?"

He paused for a second.

"I still haven't found my brother. And I wish we did because we need him."

"Your brother's in a safe place," Victor said.

"And how do you know that?" Thorn asked.

"For now, take my word for it. He knows how hectic it is out here now the child has become Dmitri's main priority. Don't stress it. For now, let's get Vegas out of here and give him what he properly deserves."

Victor and Thorn walked to the cross, proceeding to bring Vegas down. Thorn knew that despite the differences, Vegas was an angel through and through. He could only imagine what Vegas was facing in that final hour, but he knew one thing: his great friend Vegas Armano, made the ultimate sacrifice of a true soldier.

* * *

Vegas Armano's body was taken to a special space: the Lindbergh Palace. A few people gather around a spot on the ground in the backyard of the mansion where Vegas Armano was finally put to rest. Ankaro Lindbergh's place had become a safe-haven for those who loved the Lord, and at the same time, a funeral home to bring in the fallen ones.

Among the people at the funeral were Victor, Thorn, Dorian, Gloria, Shadow, and Ankaro himself. All, with the exception of Gloria, were wearing their white suits. Ankaro never wanted to see funerals as sad times, but wonderful times. It was an extravagant funeral, even though there wasn't a crowd. Despite Vegas' lifestyle and the fact that he would never be known as a true angel, Ankaro wanted to make sure that in death, he was buried as one.

Ankaro said, "Here lies a fallen soldier. He made a great sacrifice. We hope his death will not be in vain as we continue the fight to contain evil."

Thorn looked at the burial site and the closed casket that contained his friend. Then he looked up at the balcony, where he saw a familiar face. It was Cecilia, in the little beauty she had after her quarrel, with some scars on his face and drenched in covers. She put her head down and walked away. Something told Thorn from that look that she missed Vegas more than he did.

Minutes later, Cecilia went into a room and took some clothes. She roughly put them in a bag, closing it up. When she was about to leave, Thorn was standing by the door. There was no way he was going to let her leave until he got his point across. There was still love there and he wanted to find it.

"What's going on?" Thorn asked with concerned eyes.

"What are you talking about?"

"I mean, you're packing clothes. Where you going?"

Cecilia was worried. This was the first time in a while she was this close to Thorn. This time, she wasn't feeling those emotions. No love. No romance. Only contempt. However, she still had respect for him. She could never hate the man who gave her so much.

"Away!" Cecilia said. "Away from this! Away from Dmitri, the child…"

"Me?"

Cecilia paused and stared at him. "Trust me! You don't want to be near me right now. I'll only get you killed just like I did Vegas."

Thorn was sensing the tears were about to fall. He went to her and touched her shoulders. "What happened to Vegas wasn't your fault?"

Cecilia gently took his arms away. Thorn was sensing this wasn't the same Cecilia he once called his love. This Cecilia seemed stronger and colder.

"And how do you know that?" Cecilia said. "Because you said so, God's Champion? Got everything together? If I was to tell you that Vegas and I made love when you told me to watch out for him, you'll never be able to forgive me. And if you were to know what Dmitri's men did to me to try and make me talk, you'll be disgusted to even see my face. And the ironic thing about it is I sort of liked it. It was my past. Maybe Larisa was right. I'm nothing but a slut. A whore… A devil. And probably forever will be. I'm no use to you."

Cecilia finished what she was doing. Thorn went and held her gently.

"I don't think I have everything together," Thorn said. "I have my faults as well. But I forgive you. For everything. I don't care what it is. And Vegas? At this point it doesn't matter. I can't begin to get mad at you when I pushed you away. After all that and I still couldn't save my brother. But I can't let you do it again. Not this time. We need you… I need you."

Cecilia touched Thorn's considerate face. "You're sweet and generous, Thorn. I believe you're going to do some good in this world. Just don't expect me to be by your side when you do."

Cecilia released herself from Thorn's hold and walked away with her bags. Thorn sat down and covered his face with his hands. He only hoped that Cecilia didn't do anything crazy.

Shadow came in and saw Thorn. "There you are. Time to talk about the next plan of action. Where's Cecilia?"

"She's gone," Thorn said. "And I don't think she's coming back."

"She can't leave. I'll go after her."

"Let her go. She needs to think this out herself."

Shadow was impatient. "We're dealing with dangerous times here. We can't afford for her to leave like that."

"Let her go, Shadow, alright?" Thorn shouted.

Dorian, Gloria, and Victor entered as Shadow and Thorn were talking.

Dorian said, "Alright, gentlemen, we need to know what to do now. Where's Cecilia?"

"She's gone," Shadow said furiously. "And Thorn let her go."

"Let it go," Thorn said.

Victor broke the ice. "Forget her. Whatever she does at this point is on her own accord."

Dorian stood by Victor. "We have to find the couple and the child and find a way to hide them until we get rid of Dmitri."

"Dmitri is the least of your problem," Victor said. "He's a pushover. It has occurred to me that my comrades have formed an army that'll outnumber Dmitri's gang. And if you think what Dmitri did to those gangs were bad, what Erick and Kim could do will be ten times worse."

"You said that," Shadow said, "yet you still called them your comrades. After they killed innocent people and caused all this."

"Well, despite how I feel about them now, I have a connection with them that can never die."

"How do we know you won't turned on us?"

"If I did, you'll be the first one I go after."

Shadow went to Victor's face. "I would like to see you try."

Gloria came between them. "Will you give it a rest, Shadow?"

"Sorry," Shadow said. "Just want to make sure that Victor's on our side."

Victor said, "I have more at stake than you think."

"There, Shadow! You see?" Thorn said.

Dorian asked, "What do you think we should do?"

Victor glared at the door that Cecilia just left from. He waited a few seconds before answering, bringing anticipation to his new friends.

"I will lure Erick and Kim in while you guys deal with Dmitri," he said. "And Thorn can find the couple and hide them." He looked at Thorn with his dark eyes. "Are you okay with this, Thorn?"

Thorn only turned the other way, anything to avoid looking into his black eyes, which hid the face of death. Thinking about his death was a scary thought, especially since he was standing with the Black Reaper, one of the most cunning angels of death, who would make or break everything.

SHOWDOWN AT THE REAPERS' GRAVEYARD

At Larisa's request, Dmitri took her around the streets of the Tri-Cities to witness the damage done by the gang. By this time, the towns of Sodom and Gomorrah fell victim to the Underground Devils' fury. Dmitri was proud of his achievement.

"Do you believe that Vegas had the guts to go up against me?" Dmitri asked, contented. "I wouldn't have believed. And Cecilia? After all I've done for her. I knew she would soon become a traitor. They're all traitors. This is my world and they're all traitors."

Larisa put on a smile for Dmitri, thinking of her own selfish motives. She didn't care what Cecilia was or if she had died. She could rot as far as Larisa was concerned. Besides, there were more people to deal with. At one point in her life, Cecilia was the one that pushed away to another life. Larisa Rhodes was heading in that same direction.

"The world is yours, Lord Dmitri," Larisa said. "And your enemies are trembling at your feet. However, I wish I could say that things were okay, but they're not. I think that Vegas and Cecilia wouldn't be helping the child if someone pushed them to it."

"What are you saying?" Dmitri asked.

"Someone from the gang is betraying us."

"And you know who it is?"

"I'm afraid to say. It's… Giorgio Martel."

Dmitri made an abrupt stop, almost crashing. He quickly turned to Larisa. "Giorgio Martel?"

Larisa told the story.

"When we went after Vegas," she said, "after we got the upper hand on him, I saw Giorgio. Everyone was beating Vegas up. Giorgio just stood there with sadness in him, like he felt sorry for him or something. In fact, he's been acting secretive since he joined this gang. Always going away from the crowd when we have our get-togethers. Why would he do that? Then came what he did to me before. He tried to kill me when all I was trying to do was talk to him. I understand that I was a little forceful, but he had no right. That doesn't matter. The point is Giorgio knows about the child and whether he knew everything or just hiding for Vegas or Cecilia, he was an active member."

"So you're saying Giorgio knows about the child and didn't even tell us?"

"I can get him for you. Just give me the order."

Dmitri was about to say yes, but he thought of something. He trusted Giorgio. He was probably the only one of the devils he had any consideration over. Giorgio Martel reminded him of a time when he was innocent, a time where he had dreams.

"Wait a second!" Dmitri said. "I know you care about Giorgio very much. How do I know this is only to get revenge on him for not returning the favor?

"Lord Dmitri," Larisa said, "I'm loyal to this gang. And I'm loyal to the Prince of Devils. I wouldn't say this if I didn't care. Let me be loyal. Please! Let me be loyal."

Larisa went down to his waist and unfastened his pants. Dmitri closed his eyes and put his head back. Everything he was thinking before went out the window when Larisa put her mouth to his genitals. She was thinking why she should go after Giorgio when Dmitri was an easier catch.

* * *

Victor, in his black suit, was on a mission. Not only must he find the child, but also regain his name smeared by the psychotic lovers Erick and Kim. He walked the streets of the Tri-Cities to look around.

This was his scenery, the lone wolf. He loved the anticipation of surprises. That was the one thing Reapers were known for.

"I can sense them," he said to himself. "I didn't think they would come so soon."

Suddenly, Victor saw many cloaks jumping on the roofs of large buildings. Some were sliding down on them. The numbers continued to grow. Some came near Victor, but barely touched him. Some screamed taunts, but Victor thought them away. He saw the skulls that covered their faces, menacing soldiers with no direction.

"You're calling me out? You want me to follow you?"

Victor, forming into her Reaper armor and cloak, followed them, doing some of the same stunts they were doing like jumping on roofs and gliding into the night sky. Since the soldiers wanted to play, he would play, too.

And he would play for keeps.

Before he knew it, Victor landed at a place he knows too well: the Reapers' Graveyard, where Reapers were molded into death seekers. He remembered this place way too well. Other than the graveyard, he couldn't remember his past before he took the rings of the Black Reaper.

What he did remember was when he first was picked up by his mentor to become an Angel of Death. He had to be reincarnated into a soulless shadow with no allegiance to anyone but the mission of death. Since then, he had done nothing but that and became the coldest and most cunning killers.

When he rose up in ranks, he took in Erick Gold and Kim Silver, eager souls who wanted to feel what it was like, as apprentices, using the same words and taught them the same moves he learned. However, the power of seeking death came over the apprentices and death itself turned them into psychopaths. That was the first thing that Victor felt sorry for his job since he first started as a Reaper, and Victor had hardened any past feelings so he could be effective at his job.

He looked around and saw that the young Reapers were there, gawking and taunting him. They forced him into the middle of a circle. Then, Erick and Kim, with Platinum walked towards him.

"The Black Reaper," Erick said with confidence, "I figured you wanted to see what we were doing. Don't you like the outlook? I have brought more to our side than you ever did."

Kim said by Erick's side, "And soon, we'll wipe out Dmitri's army."

Victor saw the numbers. They were right. The two were able to bring more to their side and maybe more in hiding. But it didn't fade him one bit.

"So this is what it's all about now?" Victor asked. "Some war?"

"If Dmitri's going to be in our way," Kim said, "then we have to deal with the situation."

"But that brings on another problem," Erick said. "You?" He pointed at Victor. "And your new friends. You should have brought them with you."

Victor tensed up. "Really? You think I'm weaker by myself? You have more to learn."

"Look at it like this," Erick said. "I mean what can you do? Sooner or later, the students will become the teachers. Now we have a say-so in when we want that to happen."

"You'll be dead before then."

"You're so sure of yourself."

"How do you think I got far in the game if I wasn't sure?"

Erick pointed to some of the Reapers. From that, at least six Reapers came out in front of Victor, bringing out their swords. Victor smiled. He stretched out his hand and out appeared a sword.

The six attacked simultaneously. Victor defended himself, stepping back as they came closer. Then, the six separated, putting up their swords and raising their fists. Victor always liked a fistfight. All of them were in the air. Victor glided up as well. One came after him and Victor punched him. Two came after him and Victor did special moves. Victor landed back on the ground as the other four came after him from the air.

Punch after punch after kick, he was able to hurt them all. He kicked one in the air and when he was about to land on the ground, Victor spin-kick him, bending the Reaper's back and slinging him to the rest of the comrades.

A pause.

The final of the six tried to swing at him, but Victor grabbed his arm, and with all the force he could muster, he punched him so viciously, a black hole formed on the ground in which the Reaper sink into it.

With the six Reapers no match for Victor, more came out. They were at least twenty. Victor fought the same way he fought the six. Victor did not seem sidetracked by the numbers, and not only did he defeat them, he massacred them.

Erick couldn't take it anymore and jumped into the fight. He pushed the other Reaper soldiers out of the way and launched straight for Victor. Victor met him halfway and attacked first. While he was fighting him, Victor thought to himself that he improved in his fighting skills. Had he learned to channel his emotions more, Erick Gold would have taken the throne, Victor thought. Erick grabbed Victor's hand when he slipped, or Erick thought he slipped. Without noticing, Victor smiled and punched Erick as hard as he could, taking him back to his two friends.

"How's that for a fight?" Victor shouted. "You want more? I can give you more. I have all eternity."

Erick got up quickly and shook it off. Kim and Platinum took their swords out and were ready to fight while Victor just stood and stared with glimmering eyes. The crowd continued to taunt.

This went on for a few seconds until Kim and Platinum came closer to Victor as well as a wounded Erick. The two glared at one another while Kim guarded her lover. Platinum pointed her sword to Victor, and then, unexpectedly, she stabbed Erick in his heart and then, slashed Kim in her face and arm. The crowd stopped with their taunts when they saw the blow. Victor walked to Erick, holding his chest.

"I put you to rest," Victor said. "I can't let you take that child."

Victor looked at Platinum, turned, and walked away. Platinum followed him.

"What about me, master?" Platinum asked.

Victor looked at her and then at Kim, who was staggering to get up.

"Give me your sword," Victor ordered.

Platinum gave Victor the sword. Victor stabbed her in her heart.

"I send you back to your domain," he said. "You have done well."

"Thank you, master!"

Platinum fell to the ground, dead.

At that time Kim stood on her feet, shaking off the slash.

"You crazy piece of…," she said fuming. "You think this is over?"

Victor ignored and walked away slowly. Kim went to Erick and comforted him.

"I'm sorry about this," Kim said with tears in her eyes.

Erick held on to his lover tight. "Don't worry about it. I… I figured that this'll be the way I would… be taken out. Get him for me. Kill them all… for me."

"I'll do it, baby," Kim said, holding back the sadness. "I'll do it for you."

Erick died in her arms. Kim cried on her chest. The other Reapers cry with her as Victor was out of sight by this time. She slowly got up and stared at the other Reapers.

"Now, it's time for war. We're going to find this child… I don't care if we have to burn everything around us. Find that child and take care of Victor and his friends."

The Reapers cheered. Then, the army lined up. They started marching from the graveyard, skulls in appearance, and no emotion, only for achieving death.

Their destination was the Tri-Cities. No mercy would be given. Kim Silver was about to show all of Greenwood's creatures the true meaning of the word death.

MARQUIS TOWERS

Robin was on the phone with someone.

"Get out of there while you can," she said. "Please, do it!"

Larisa entered with a bag in her hand and Robin quickly put the phone down and acted like she was doing something else.

"What's going on, little sis?" Larisa asked strangely.

"Nothing," Robin said.

"There's something I have to show you."

Larisa took out some money and put it to Robin's face.

"What is this?" Robin asked, not appreciating what she's doing.

"A gift from Lord Dmitri to you."

Then came the anger. "What makes you think I want something from you or your pimp?"

"He's my new sponsor," Larisa said. "A big difference. And besides, you need it. And I want to make sure my nephew is taken care of."

"My son will be taken care of."

Larisa matched the range of Robin's shouting with some of her own. "You know, after all I've done for you and all you can do is talk to me like I don't exist."

Robin was livid. She tried not to get to this place again, but she was tired of Larisa. "After what you've done for me? What have you done for me? You treated our parents like crap when they were living. You almost tried to kill me. And you want to talk about how you've been treated? As far as I'm concerned, I don't have a sister. I never did. You're a disgrace!"

Robin walked out of the room and into another. Larisa held her anger in for someone who went off the loose end in a second. She went to her nephew, who was sound asleep in his crib.

She picked him up and looked at him. A grin came upon her face. She felt better when she held her nephew.

If only her mother would, she thought.

"Aren't you the cutest thing in the world? I don't know why Robin treats me like this when I'm doing this for her and you."

Larisa stared at the child and started thinking.

Wait a second!

All this time, Larisa was searching for babies, but one she didn't even looked at was her own nephew. Another idea came in her mind, a twisted one. She knew that with this idea, she could take revenge on everyone and everything.

Could you... be the one?

Larisa looked to see if Robin was coming back. Larisa slowly took her nephew and walked out the door. Robin came back to see if the child was there. Robin saw that the child and Larisa were gone.

* * *

Larisa drove a car with Robin's child on the passenger's side. She took out a phone, dialed a number, and put it to her ear.

"Lord Dmitri, this is Larisa. I have good news for you. I've found him... No joke. Trust me, this is the real deal... Meet me at the Marquis Towers near the Tri-Cities... I just want to make sure I'm not followed by anyone... Alright, I'll wait for you."

She put the phone up and glared at the child, who was right by her. The child had now become her ticket to a change life.

"Who would have believed that you were here the whole time and I didn't see it?" Larisa said.

Then, something else came into her mind. Something told her that it wasn't her considering, but the child thinking for her. Perhaps this was the power.

"Wait a minute! Why should I let Lord Dmitri have this child? You're my blood. Don't worry! If you have power like they say you do, you'll take care of all my enemies."

Like her mind, the car started going full speed. Larisa told herself that what better place to take care of all her enemies than to the Marquis Towers.

* * *

Dmitri put down the phone at his office when Essence, Slash, and Giorgio came in.

"Larisa has found the child," Dmitri said immediately.

"Are you sure?" Essence asked.

"She seems sure. Besides, I trust Larisa."

"When did this happen?"

Slash asked, "What you want to do?"

"Gather the soldiers," Dmitri ordered. "We're going to the Marquis Towers."

Essence was traumatized. "Marquis Towers? Are you crazy? I heard that place is haunted.

"This is more important that some spooks," Dmitri said. "Besides, this is the land of our master. We practically lived there. Now, get ready with anything and everything just in case we have to deal with an army."

"We're going to have watched Larisa."

Slash smirked. "I thought that was your girl."

"I thought so, too. But something tells me Larisa's living her own route."

Essence, Slash, and Giorgio walked away. Dmitri grabbed Slash's arm and pulled him to a corner.

"Have you noticed something weird about Giorgio?" Dmitri asked, thinking about the last conversation he had with Larisa.

"What you mean?" Slash wondered.

"Larisa told me that Giorgio had something to do with hiding the child."

"And you believe her?"

"Why should she lie? Look, watch Giorgio. He slips once, get rid of him."

Slash left as Dmitri smiled in success. He may have trusted Giorgio, but he didn't trust the notion of betrayal in his circle.

* * *

Robin opened the door to her house for Thorn, who looked around. He ignored the fact that she had been crying.

"We have to get out of here," Thorn said in a hurry. "Where's your child?"

Robin was angry, which hid the grief well. "Larisa took her."

"Why would she do that?"

"Larisa works for Dmitri. I should have told you, but I thought she could change. I should have known better."

Thorn paused. "Why would you say that?"

"Or maybe it's something else. I mean, she always hated our mother and me ever since we were kids. Then again, I don't know."

"Just what we need. Look, do you have any idea where she might go?"

A knock was on the door. Thorn went to the door cautiously. He opened it, manhandling the person who came in and pushed him to the floor, ready to punch him. It was Giorgio. Robin got Thorn off of him and helped him up. Robin and Giorgio hugged each other hard.

"So glad to see you," Robin said joyfully.

"We have to go to Marquis Towers," Giorgio said. "Larisa has our child. How did you let her get him?"

"I didn't think she knew he was special," Robin said. "But she knows now, and is going to use him for her advantage."

Giorgio wanted to tell her about it. He knew Larisa and Robin were sisters, which was the main reason why he stayed away from her.

Instead, Giorgio said, "Not if I have anything to say about that."

Thorn said, "I'll let the rest of the guys know. You're not fighting this battle alone.

Thorn took out a phone, dialed a number, and talked in it. "Dorian. This is Thorn. Dmitri's gang is going to Marquis Towers. They have the child. Meet us there."

Then, Thorn, Giorgio, and Robin left the safety of Robin's home for the dangerous Marquis Towers.

* * *

The Marquis Towers were the pride of the Tri-Cities. They stood as a reminder that once upon a time, there was chaos in Greenwood.

Now, the two long-stem towers, named *Power* and *Glory*, stood as monuments of a time passed and a future hanging in the balance.

On a dark night like this, it became a haunting sight.

The beings of Greenwood that built the towers were looking for two things. One was a reminder that evil still existed. The other was more complex. It was to show that although hate and evil existed, it kept balance together with the benevolent and good, and the children of Greenwood should strive to go the right path.

Dmitri and the Underground gang marched, heading for the two towers with a small bridge between them. They crossed a massive bridge from one city and went through small towns. Everyone who watched knew what was about to happen, and no one dare crossed their path. Thunder started roaring and lightning flashed. All of Dmitri's gang had strange looks when staring at the towers. Closer and closer they went, it got larger and larger. However, Dmitri smiled. Essence walked to Dmitri.

"Massive," Dmitri said, admiring the sight.

"And Larisa is here," Essence said. "I don't like this. What if something there wants to get us?"

"I know you're not getting scared. Let's get in and out."

With Dmitri leading the way, the gang went inside one of the large towers, the Power Tower.

* * *

Looking from a window at the Glory Tower was Larisa. As far as she was concerned, with her nephew beside her, she had control of the situation

That's right. Come to Larisa.

The child started crying and Larisa tended to him.

"Come on, come on," Larisa whispered. "You have to keep quiet. You want my plan to work, don't you? When it's all said and done, it'll be just you and me. I promise. You'll be my son."

Larisa walked back to the window. Then, she saw Thorn, Giorgio, and Robin coming to the gate.

"What's this? My sister's here? How does she know I was here?"

Larisa looked at Giorgio and how close he was with Robin.

"Giorgio? What is she doing with my sister?"

Larisa paused and then put her head down. Then, she put her head up and gazed at the child.

She was shocked. The one thing she didn't comprehend was how the boy's face looked liked Giorgio's.

"No! It can't be. Giorgio… he is…? It makes sense now. That's why he won't…"

Suddenly, Larisa screamed, took out a gun and started shooting near the child, with no harm coming to him.

* * *

Thorn, Giorgio, and Robin walked on to the Power Tower.

"When the rest of your friends coming?" Giorgio asked.

"They should be coming any minute now," Thorn said.

Noises were heard. Robin was the first to notice.

"Someone's following us," she said.

Giorgio stood by Robin, making sure he was keeping a close eye on her as close as he could.

"Are you sure?" he asked.

All three searched around and saw only shadows of unknown objects. Then, Giorgio was punched by someone with quick speed and fell to the ground. The colossal Slash appeared from the shadows before them, closer to Giorgio than the rest of them.

"Traitor!" Slash shouted.

"Slash," Giorgio said as he comforted Robin.

Thorn stood in front of Giorgio and Robin.

"Giorgio, you and Robin find your son," he said.

Slash took some time to think. "Son? That's why you betrayed us? Your son will be mine. That should be payment for your betrayal."

"He's not giving you anything," Thorn said.

"Too bad. Then all of you will die. And I have no problem with that."

"Get out of here." Thorn shouted to the couple as loud as he could.

Thorn brought out a long sword from his back. Slash brought out metallic claws and tried to attack, but Thorn stopped him and the two fought. The two were fighting like raging bulls. Neither one knew what kind of force they could create.

Robin and Giorgio ran away while the two huge men struggle like wrestlers in a ring.

In Thorn's eyes, Slash was not as quick as with Victor's henchmen, but certainly tougher. Thorn got the upper hand when he took his sword and stabbed Slash in the heart. Slash fell dead. Thorn turned around to catch his breath. Slash quickly got up and was about to kill Thorn, but five holes went through Slash's body and he fell dead, this time for good. Thorn turned to see a dead Slash near him and Shadow Fades standing at a distance.

"I did it right this time," Shadow said. "Where Robin and Giorgio?"

"They went to find the baby," Thorn said.

Dorian and Gloria entered and join Thorn and Shadow.

"There you are," Dorian said. "Other angels know where we are."

"You brought an army?" Thorn asked, energetic at the turn of events.

Shadow said, "Robin and Giorgio went on their own."

"In this crazy place?" Gloria said. "They don't know what dangers are here."

The sounds of running became louder and louder stomps. Shadow knew who they were.

"Dmitri's gang must know were here," he said.

Dorian hollered, "We have to go now."

The alliance ran on.

* * *

Robin and Giorgio went into a dark room.

"What did we walk up on?" Robin asked, holding on to Giorgio's arm tight.

"I don't know."

Sounds of crying were heard.

"I hear him," Robin said. "We're coming, baby!"

Robin was running the other way, but ran into Essence's strong fists. She fell to the ground, and went after Giorgio with a knife. Giorgio was able to move away from the blade swiftly.

"I knew you were a traitor," Essence said.

Giorgio was not a fighter, but he tried to play a good game anyway.

"You will not harm my son," he said.

"Your son is the least of your problems."

Essence beat down Giorgio with her fists. Giorgio fell to the ground. She was about to kill Giorgio, but then a familiar face stabbed her in her shoulder. Essence fell to her knees holding her shoulder, with a battle-ready Cecilia standing behind her. Giorgio was amazed.

"I told your friend that I'd get you all back," Cecilia said. "Think I was lying to you? Giorgio, get out of here. Find your son."

Giorgio said, "Follow us as soon as you can."

He got up and ran away.

An injured Essence tried to get up. "What… are you…"

"Doing here?" Cecilia said finishing her sentence. "I was going to get back at your sister-in-arms, but I guess you'll have to come close."

"You think this will all end when you get rid of me? You're still going to be a reject. They'll never accept you. Face it! You'll still be a little slut."

"I'm not looking for acceptance now."

"And you have another problem on your hands."

Essence took out another knife and stabbed Cecilia in the arm. "Don't think I'll go out that easy."

Essence and Cecilia fought. The struggle went on until Essence got around her in a bear-hug maneuver, squeezing her very tight.

"You know, before you die," Essence said. "I have to say, I never really like you. Always trying to look better than everyone else with your pretty face. I like nothing better than to rearrange it. That would make me feel so better."

Cecilia tried to talk. "Well… I have to say that I always love you as a sister. And I always will. But… I must do this."

Suddenly, Cecilia released her hold and quickly stabbed herself, but the sword was long enough to go through her and Essence's heart. Essence walked slowly back, holding her blooded heart, and collapse. Cecilia, staggering, went to her. She touched Essence's face.

"Now, we'll go back to hell together."

Cecilia lied near Essence and fell dead.

* * *

Giorgio and Robin came into a luxurious room in the Power Tower. It was unusual for an old tower to have wealthy rooms, another great masterpiece done by its designers.

"What is this?" Robin asked.

"This whole place is crazy," Giorgio said. "I don't understand any of this."

Suddenly, they looked at a door that opened up by itself and standing there was Larisa, who pointed a gun at them.

"Welcome," Larisa said with a considerate look, hiding the treachery within. "Didn't think you'll get so far."

Robin came out in anger. "Where's my child, you bitch?"

Larisa shot at her, missing her by inches.

"Don't you even dare get mad at me," she said. "After what you've done to me, you think I'm telling you anything?" She looked at Giorgio. "And you! I'm really disappointed at you. So this is why you didn't want anything to do with me? You're with my sister this whole time. Once again, my sister gets everything."

Then, a fellow soldier of Dmitri walked in with the child in his hands. Robin tried to run to it, but Giorgio stopped her.

"What are you trying to prove here?" Giorgio asked.

"Play with my feelings," Larisa said, "and I'll play with yours."

The soldier left with the child. Larisa started shooting around. Giorgio took Robin to the ground, covering her. When they got up, Larisa ran out the door. Giorgio went after her.

* * *

Dmitri was running from Shadow. It was a shootout between the two sharpshooters. Shadow ran to a certain point and lost Dmitri. He went inside another corner of the Power Tower. He looked slowly around in the dark. The darkness inside and the night outside was confusing him. Then, he heard noise. He quickly turned around and pointed his gun at shadows. The shadows emerged into Reapers, led by a scared-face Kim Silver.

Kim gave the order. "Kill him."

The Reapers shot with their guns at Shadow, mercilessly killing him. Kim walked slowly over his body and stabbed him to make sure he was dead. She walked on with her soldiers following her.

* * *

Larisa ran onto the bridge connecting the Towers as far as she could. Lightning was flashing quicker than usual, almost hitting the bridge. When she reached the end, Giorgio ran on it.

"Larisa stop!" Giorgio yelled.

Larisa stopped and turned, with the gun pointing at him. She started walking forward. "Don't you dare try to stop me, Giorgio," she said. You lost that right!"

"Larisa, don't do this," Giorgio pleaded. "If you want to harm somebody, harm me, okay? I'm to blame for this. Just let us talk about this."

There was a pause.

Larisa was looking into Giorgio's beautiful eyes. At this point, she still couldn't resist them.

"Giorgio Martel, you're really charming," she said. "But… you're not that charming. Vengeance must be taken, and I will have mine."

"It's me you want."

"You know… you're right about this. This is your fault… One more thing. I belong to Dmitri now. He's my savior."

Suddenly, a shot was heard. Giorgio covered his head. Larisa looked at herself and saw a small hole in her arm. She turned and saw her sister Robin, pointing the gun at her with the same heartlessness with a purpose.

"Where's my child, Larisa?" Robin said.

Larisa laughed crazily. "Do you think that I'm going to tell you where that child is? You must be crazy. The secret will die with me."

Larisa was about to shoot, but Robin shot first. The bullet got Larisa in the chest. This made her lose her balance and she fell off the bridge and below the Towers. Tears came down Robin's eyes. Giorgio rushed to her and hugged her tight, kissing her on the forehead.

* * *

Thorn dashed into a room where there were paintings of black angels.

Dmitri strolled in. "Thorn!" he shouted.

Thorn circled around. "Finally!"

"Well, do you want to start this?" Dmitri asked. "Prepare to join your friend and your brother."

"That'll be the biggest mistake of your life."

Thorn launched after Dmitri and the two clashed. During the fight, Thorn brought out his sword and so did Dmitri. A fistfight became a sword fight. A few minutes into the fight, Dmitri injured Thorn and he fell back. Dmitri moved forward and knocked the sword from his hand.

"You must be crazy if you thought I was going to be a pushover," Dmitri said.

Dmitri was about to strike, but a knife stuck him in his hand. He revolved around while holding his hand to see who it was.

It was Victor Marcus, holding his Reaper sword. "Get out of here, Thorn! This is my fight now."

Thorn slowly got up, picked up his sword and strolled off.

"Thanks, Victor," Thorn said.

"No problem."

Dmitri laughed. "Well, well!" he said. "Victor Marcus. The Black Reaper. I've heard stories about you. Your legend is extraordinary. Who would have thought you'll be involved in this?"

Intensity was in the eyes of Victor Marcus. It showed that he was going to have fun in hating this person.

"Dmitri Sheppard," Victor said, "you have just live your last days here."

"Is that right?" Dmitri said not amused. "Well, I must say, I don't think so. In fact, my days of carnage are just beginning. And what better way to show my fury than by defeating the Black Reaper himself."

Dmitri clinched his fist and his whole body started to shake. Light and darkness surrounded his body and it was growing larger and larger. The floor shook within. Despite all the effects,

Victor remained motionless with the same cool look. Dmitri finished, with more power in him than ever before. It was time to see if his practice in the Dark Arts was worth it.

Victor grinned. "Is that it? Great!"

Dmitri was shocked. Victor was amusing himself on Dmitri's expense. Then spontaneously, Victor screamed. His scream was so loud, it took Dmitri and other objects back, almost falling off the Towers, but it was not to be thanks to Dmitri's balance.

Victor started laughing. "That… is power. Impressed? I hope so, because that was only a taste of what you're about to experience."

Victor was appearing into his Reaper armor and cloak.

Despite the pain he felt, Dmitri laughed. "I'll admit. That was impressive. But it's time to really show you what I'm made of."

Dmitri charged at him with great speed. He managed to get halfway when Victor disappeared, leaving parts of his cape behind. He reappeared behind him and Dmitri swung his fist, missing him. Dmitri circled around, trying to find him.

"Don't you understand, Dmitri," Victor said. "No hope is there for you."

Dmitri was getting impatient. "Come on out and fight me."

Suddenly, Dmitri was being punched by thin air. Dmitri swung his fist, but he was no match for Victor's powers when he was invisible. He fell back to the floor. More punch and kicks pushed Dmitri back and forth like a ragdoll. Dmitri slowly got up from the floor, but was taken into the air. Victor reappeared, with his hand on his neck.

Dmitri was in agony. "What… what is this all about? About the child… About Vegas…"

Victor's eyes were turning dark. Part of his face was disappearing as he was coming toward Dmitri. It was becoming a skull. A few people saw his true form, but none lived to tell about it.

"This isn't about the child or Vegas," Victor said. "I'm doing this because I just don't like you. I've been waiting to shut your mouth up for a long time." He put his face closer so Dmitri could get a good look. "Unfortunately… I have personal business to deal with."

Victor dropped Dmitri on the floor. He came down and walked forward. Dmitri crawled to get his sword. He got up and charged after him. Victor stuck out his hands and Dmitri ran into it. He stopped ahead and turned around. Victor stood motionless. Dmitri smiled and before Victor's eyes, his body was torn to pieces. Victor walked to his dissembled body and stuck out his hand. Some visible red dust, Dmitri's soul, landed into Victor's hand and from that, he closed it.

"You soul is mine now, Dmitri Sheppard."

* * *

Dorian and Gloria ended the fight with the rest of Dmitri's men. It was a gruesome fight, but a fight they had no choice but to face. When it was done, Gloria gestured a cross in front of the men who laid a bloody mess. They were at the Glory Tower. Thorn entered and joined them.

Dorian said happily, "Thorn! Where are the others?"

"I don't know," Thorn said. "Victor was fighting Dmitri."

Robin and Giorgio entered. Noises of crying were heard.

"I hear him again," Robin said.

Robin started running to the sounds of crying. The rest of them followed her.

Robin went into another secret room, darker and more gruesome than the other insignificant rooms. Lying in a comfortable basket at a corner was Giorgio and Robin's son. Giorgio and the others came in and saw the child.

"I don't like this," Dorian said, circling around. "The shadows seemed to be moving."

Robin ran to the child, but when she only got a few feet close, a sword landed near Robin, almost cutting her foot off. Coming out from the large room were the Reapers, with Kim Silver standing on top of a platform. The Reapers surrounded the group. Kim jumped off the platform and landed near the child.

"No!" Robin shouted.

Kim blew a kiss. "Too late, darling! Your child is mine now."

"Let go of my son," Giorgio said, clinching his fists.

"Well, I know now who the parents are. With that in mind, Reapers… kill them all."

The Reapers struck the group and a battle emerged. Kim escaped out from the room. Robin ran after her. Giorgio, after dealing with some of the Reapers as best he can, ran after them.

Kim made it to the roof of Glory Tower. She held the child in the air as it was crying.

"Give me the power!" Kim roared. "Mighty angel, give me the power!"

Robin entered and rushed to Kim, but Kim, noticing the footsteps, punched her to the ground with one of her fists. Kim put the child near the roof, away from the women. Kim paced slowly to her.

"Did you think that you could attack me like that," Kim said. "Face it, your child's a treasure. I possess it now. And I'll kill anyone who crosses me. Even an innocent like you."

Kim was about to strike, but Giorgio jumped in and saved her the trouble. Giorgio and Kim fought, but Giorgio was no match for Kim and her fast moves. Robin was able to get up and, taking a sword she found on the ground, she swung it, being able to put a scar on Kim's shoulder. Robin stepped back. Kim stared at her wound. More anger was fueling in her at the site of Robin, standing ready with the sword in her hand. No mere mortal were able to put a scar in her.

"Nice," Kim said confidently at the site of a wound. "So you do have some fight in you?"

Giorgio got up and jumped into the fight again. Kim knocked out Giorgio again. Robin tried to run to her, but Kim grabbed her arm, making her drop her sword, and held on to her, with a knife to her neck.

"Isn't this nice," Kim said sinisterly. "All this for your child. Why risk it? You and your boyfriend will just be dead and the child will still be mine. Why deal with the pressure?"

Victor appeared suddenly and Kim was shaken up.

"Victor!"

Kim held on tighter to Robin.

"Using a little girl as your shield," Victor said. "Running out of originality, darling!"

Kim threw Robin to the side and came out swinging her fists at Victor. She was fighting so quickly that Victor had to bring out his sword and finished it then and there if he ever had a chance. Kim brought out a sword from her head and the fight became even. Kim had more fight than Erick did. The force the two Reapers were bringing out amazed Robin and Giorgio, who were separated from each other.

It was worse than the storm, Giorgio thought.

Victor was able to give a blow to Kim on her breastplate that really stunned her. She walked back slowly, holding her breast. Then, she grabbed Robin, trying to get to her son, by the arm and once again, put the knife to her neck.

"Back to that again," Victor said. "I thought you were going to put up a fight. It comes to show you that you still have much to learn."

"Go ahead," Kim said. "Try to kill me. You'll be killing her as well."

"Like I care about her! If it's her time, then it's her time."

"No you don't! You're not playing that game with me."

Victor strolled a few steps and Kim walked back.

"Don't do it," Kim said, hoping Victor would stop.

"Kill her," Victor stressed. "I dare you!"

Suddenly, Giorgio attacked and Kim kicked him. Victor took the sword from the ground near her and threw it to Robin. Robin grabbed it and swung it. Kim moved quick enough from the sword reaching her head, but Robin was able to slit Kim's throat. Kim held on to her neck tight, but staggered to the floor. With the little life in her, she backed away to the end of the tower.

Robin dropped the sword, with the blood tainted on her hand. She headed for Victor and hugged him hard. Giorgio got up and Robin hugged her. The couple went to their child that was near Kim's body and comforted him.

Victor watched them carefully. Then, he went to Kim, who was still moving. She was staring at Victor, trying her best to regain some energy. Victor knew that she would be a danger if she ever came back alive. So, he took her sword and with one swipe, decapitated her head.

A SURPRISE AND A WARNING

THE ALLIANCE WENT BACK TO ANKARO'S HOME. AFTER THE HORRENDOUS battle they fought with the Underground Devils and the Reapers, they were relieved, even more if they never have to walk inside Marquis Towers again. Robin and Giorgio comforted their child with the best care. Thorn, Dorian, and Gloria watched them with the sweetest eyes. It was happy to see the small family in the young lovers.

Victor, covered in his black cloak, was alone at a corner, but dragged himself to them. Something in him wished that he could express the same happiness everyone else was showing, but his duty would not let him, even for a few seconds.

"Look at them," Dorian said. "Nice couple,"

"Thank God, it's all over," Thorn said.

Victor stared at him strangely. "No!"

"You said something, Victor?" Thorn asked.

Victor's eyes went to the couple. "It's not over, yet. There's something else that must be done and right now."

"What else needs to be done?"

All eyes were on Victor. He took a couple of steps. The cape went around Victor and he took out a gun swiftly, pointing it at the child.

Thorn took a couple steps back. All were in shock. Victor stood like a statue, cold and menacing as he was with his former apprentices.

"What are you doing?" Thorn asked.

"The child…" Victor said. "The child must die, Thorn. It will not be over unless it's done."

"I don't understand."

He kept his attention to the couple. "Robin… Giorgio… I know you care about this child, but for the sake of your planet, step away from the child, for if you don't… I fear I would have to sacrifice you as well."

Dorian came in the picture. "Victor, stop this. This isn't funny."

"It's not meant to be funny," Victor said.

"What are you saying?" Gloria asked.

"You must understand that I'm doing something right for a change. Too many people have died just to claim this child. And before anything worse happens, I will take the initiative."

Dorian and Gloria stepped back. Thorn stepped in a little. Giorgio and Robin held on to the child closely. In Robin's mind, she knew that there was something extraordinary about her child. Dmitri and his gang wanted it. The Reapers was willing to betray and kill anyone for it. Larisa stole it from her home for it. And seeing Victor Marcus talking about killing their child because it caused deaths, confirmed that notion.

Victor continued, his attention going to Thorn, but keeping a close eye on the couple.

"But I must say, Thorn, I should thank you for this. I was able to get this far because of your determination. I sense you had it then when I sent my henchman to attack you at the locker."

Thorn was a little surprised. He had forgotten about his henchman.

Victor continued. "I knew you would defeat him. I have planned it all to a tee and I had used them all. The pact of Vegas and Cecilia. Dmitri's involvement. The betrayal of my comrades. I used them to get this far, but then, their own personal feelings got in the way and were about to ruin it all. Then, you came along and seize the rings."

"Why are you doing this to an innocent child?" Thorn asked. "A baby, for goodness sake?"

"This is more than a mere baby," Victor shouted angrily. "This child will grow up to become one of the most destructive beings on the face of this world."

Thorn walked closer to Victor.

"A harbinger of chaos?" Dorian asked.

"Worse than that," Victor said.

Thorn was running out of ideas. He didn't know what to do. He knew that one day, when he was older and ready to face the end, he would face Victor again. This was a different story, however.

"All my life," Victor said, "I have never done anything right with this world. Now, I have the chance to redeem myself. Well… if you don't think about that, then think about this. 'You give me a devil of creation, and I will give you an angel of destruction.'"

Dorian and Gloria were surprised. He knew the words as well.

"The last words of the Prince of Devils before he broke his hold on the Old World. Most thought of it as a joke. Well, now it could come to pass if I don't stop now."

Thorn got in Victor's way.

"Get out my way if you know what is good for you," Victor said as the gun went closer to Thorn's chest.

Thorn stretched out his hands. "Do what you want, but I will not let you kill this child."

Victor was getting frustrated, the first time Thorn saw it. All that time, he thought of Victor as a being in control of everything. Now he was seeing Victor as a maniac that could lose control any minute.

"Why are you doing this?" Victor asked. "Knowing well that when this child grows up, it'll become a chaotic machine. It will kill you. All of you!"

"It's just a little baby right now," Thorn said. "It can't harm anyone. And you have two loving parents that care much for that child to make sure nothing happens to it. I will not let you kill this child. Sacrifice me for the child."

"And what makes you think they would live that long?"

"I'll just have to put my faith in my Lord. What more is there to do?"

Victor showed his teeth as he raised the gun to Thorn's head. There was a pause. The alliance grasped. Thorn was slowly reaching for it. Before he could, Victor slowly put the gun down.

"Thank you," Thorn said as he took a breath of relief.

Victor was not grateful.

"Don't thank me," he said. "As far as I'm concerned, for all who are in this room, you're all dead."

"We have a chance to stop it from happening, if it's true," Thorn said.

Another pause. All were thinking of what transpired. Victor recovered himself with his black cloak, back to his restraint.

"One condition will make me be okay with this," Victor said. "When the child reaches his tenth year, I will take him under my wing. Do not fight me on this. This will happen whether you want it or not. At least that way, if it happens, I'll take care of it before it becomes a problem. As of this point, all of you… are no longer trustworthy."

Victor walked away, possibly forever in the alliance's eyes. Thorn tried to chase after him, but Dorian stopped him.

"He must deal with this himself," Dorian whispered.

Thorn looked at Victor as he slowly disappeared. Then, he looked at Giorgio and Robin.

"I wander was it a mistake?" Dorian asked.

"What could we do," Gloria said. "Victor Marcus is already dead."

* * *

Weeks went by since the battle at Marquis Towers. Times became happier. The Angel Guards sought the remaining Underground Devils. In the end, with no one to lead or guide them, most died mysteriously.

The Reapers were put in their place for the time being.

And now, in a church built by Ankaro Lindbergh, the young lovers, the angel and the devil, Giorgio and Robin Martel walked with their child up to the podium when Ankaro took the child from them, held it in his arms and raised it to the air.

Ankaro said, "The Lord bless this child, Vegas Victor Martel, as well as the parents, Mr. and Mrs. Giorgio Martel."

Everyone stood up and cheered for them, including the old alliance that included Dorian, Gloria, and Thorn. Thorn, who became the child's godfather, went to the couple and hugged them both.

* * *

Victor Marcus was staring forward, standing on the roof of the Power Tower of Marquis Towers. After fighting his own soldiers and helping the angels and dealing with his conscience for once because of the angelic Thorn Hawkins, he was facing conflicting thoughts.

"Am I doing the right thing?" Victor said to himself.

Suddenly, The Marquis Red entered and stood to Victor's side.

"It's okay to be a little concerned," Red said. "They should have listened to you. Or should I say, you should have taken that initiative."

"You know," Victor said as he turned to look at him. "The one thing I have to hate the Lord for… is not getting rid of you when he had the chance."

"It's such a shame. Even when I haven't done anything, I'm still blame for misery in the world."

Red went to Victor's ear.

"Well, note this," he said. "When it becomes true, it will not be my fault. My hands will be clean. All I will do is sit and wait. Wait for his reign to fall. He'll need me again. Besides, what will the world be like… without the Prince of Devils?"

The Marquis walked away, but stopped.

"Guess what they named the child," he said. "Vegas Victor Martel! Name for the one who died for the child and the one… who spared him from death itself."

The Marquis walked away, laughing.

"Vegas Victor Martel! The angel of destruction! I fear only the worse."

Victor put his head down. Then, he looked at the sky, thinking the whole time.

Why couldn't the rest of them just listen to him when he had the chance? What would he be able to do if they did? Could he regret ever killing this child, a child with the characteristics of an angel and a devil, a root of good and a root of evil?

Victor went back to the Reaper's Graveyard. He looked at the grave, full of the sleeping Reapers ready to sprout their wings. For once, Victor was depressed at coming back here after what he had done. He let the child live. He failed his mission. He went on one knee and touched a part of the burial ground. He took a taste of it with his lips and like the hourglass, put his hand into a fist and let the dirt go down his hand smoothly.

Then, surprisingly, Victor's large henchman and a mysterious Reaper that was taken it not too long ago came to him. The henchman touched Victor's shoulder.

"Are you okay?" the henchman asked.

"I don't know," Victor said. I really don't know."

Suddenly, Victor raised himself up. He turned his head left and right.

"Who is it?" The henchman said.

"Someone else is here."

Then, he heard it.

You failed, Victor.

Victor recognized the voices.

You failed, Victor.

Victor took out his sword. The mysterious Reaper took out his and the henchman raised his fists.

You failed, Victor.

Then, Victor saw him. Four Reapers appeared from the distance, not showing their faces. The Absolute Four. The Reaper Knights, the main guards for the Grim Reaper.

Zakros said that you have failed, Victor.

The henchman was sensing Victor's uneasiness.

"Well, you tell Zakros that I'll talk to him later," Victor said.

With that, the four disappeared. Victor walked away from his two apprentices.

"What now?" The mysterious Reaper asked, breaking his silence.

"Something tells me that things are going to get worse before it ever gets better," Victor said and put his sword away. "I must be alone. Don't wait up for me."

With that, Victor left the graveyard, while the two Reapers wondered.

That night, Victor Marcus walked the streets of the Tri-Cities alone, like he always had been. No apprentices or friends with him, which he liked. At this point in time, he needed the loneliness. He needed to plan the rest of his existence on what might become the greatest and most treacherous years of the lives of his new acquaintances.

He thought of the image, the child, the angel of destruction, and the future man who would make or break Greenwood.

Angels and devils will bow before him.

All would fear him.

Some will attack him.

Few will succeed.

One knows it all. Could he stop it?

That… was for another time, another time that Victor Marcus's so-called Reaper heart would have to seek out…

Printed in the United States
by Baker & Taylor Publisher Services